cold, thin air

volume 4

C.K. Walker

IBSN: 9781076960528

c.k.walker

For the fans:

To whom I owe everything and always will.

TABLE OF CONTENTS

The Boy in the Alley

I can't tell you how many times I'd seen him. Maybe a hundred times, over the last nine months or so. He was just a boy - much younger than me, maybe nine year old, if I was forced to guess. Though, he could have been older; that's how malnourished he was.

I didn't know his name, and I never asked. Even though I was sure that I *knew* him as soon as I saw him, I couldn't possibly have. This boy and I would *not* have run in the same circles. It didn't really matter, anyway, he was just "the boy", in my head. Skinny, gaunt. Runt. His hair looked like it hadn't been washed in months and it probably hadn't been. Maybe not even in years. And the boy, he smelled, too. Stunk actually... Still, that wasn't his fault and I did what I could for him.

The first time I saw him was in March. I owed my friend money for a bar tab from spring break. A bar tab, I might add, that got absolutely out of control that night. We were in Miami for the week, Amanda, three of our other friends, and me. I kept taking the drinks, but I wasn't the one ordering them. I didn't even want them. I took them to be polite. Eventually, I drove home by myself because they refused to leave. I didn't want those drinks, but *still* Amanda wanted me to pay. It had been her card behind the bar.

But, luckily, she didn't have my schedule for that semester so she couldn't stalk me on campus. She did, however, know where I lived and sometimes she'd wait in my lobby to catch me and hound me for her $230 dollars. I told her I hadn't even wanted the damn drinks *and* I had left earlier than the rest of our group. Still, she wanted me to pay. I'd left them stranded at the bar without a car. She was pissed. I told her I was drunk and tired, and they wouldn't leave. She said that was no excuse. So I owed her the money.

Amanda's family is richer than mine so I don't understand why she put so much energy into getting the $230 dollars. But she did.

For that reason, and that reason alone, I started using the backdoor of my complex. I didn't want to be ambushed by Amanda again. It was embarrassing! The back door was only accessible from the filthy alley behind the building, but I was desperate.

I saw him the first day I used the back entrance. He was sitting against the wall, covered in ratty clothing and staring down at his hands. And he had a little cup with holes it in set in front of him. You know, the kind you get from casinos and arcades. This one said "Palm Coast Games" on it in dark blue. Such a little cup. And so empty.

I don't know why the boy wasn't out on a main street, where people could see him and put money in his little, hole-y cup. Maybe he was hiding from someone. Or maybe he just wanted some respite from the sharp, spring wind that snaked through the city, tearing coffee cups and train tickets out of frigid fingers.

But, for whatever reason, that's where he was - against the wall in my dirty alley, hidden away from everyone, including Amanda. Everyone but me. So there we are - two stowaways from reality, hiding in the filth.

I tried to walk by him without looking that first time. But I couldn't help it. He was such a small, scraggly thing. The boy caught my eye, and you know, once they look at you it's so hard to keep on walking by, ignoring them.

So, he caught me unaware, made eye contact with me, and then watched as I dug into my purse and pulled out the few dollar bills I had. I didn't carry cash very often, because cash is dirty. People don't wash their hands or they clothes as often as they should; there are germs all over every dollar bill you see. That's the nature of paper currency. I prefer plastic, to be honest, so I rarely have cash.

See? I wasn't lying to Amanda about that. I don't like cash. I never had any when she came by. Hell, I'd barely had enough on me to get the car out of valet that night.

I dropped the few bills into his cup. He didn't say anything, so I didn't either. I kept walking and went upstairs. I slept well that night. It's nice to do something for someone else.

When I came back down the next morning, I used the alley door again. The boy was still there but the money in his hole-y cup was gone. We didn't make eye contact that morning, so I just walked by.

The boy wasn't there all the time, but I always tried to have some coins in my purse to drop into his cup for when he was, just in case we made accidental eye contact. Sometimes I don't think he even wanted it. Because he didn't always look up at me.

Some days he just stared down at his filthy, mismatched shoes, or his grubby hands. He tried to hide them from me, but I saw. I knew he was embarrassed. And as the weeks went on, I noticed he only looked at me for eye contact when he seemed truly desperate.

That made me sad. I put more money in his cup when I was feeling sad. That made us both feel better. We were connected that way.

Summer rolled in and my boy took to wearing less clothing because of the heat. I'd still bring him spare change when he caught my eye. It was a sweltering summer so I even started bringing him the half empty water bottles that sat in my car during the hottest months. I think he appreciated that, and it made me feel good, too. One time, I even brought one down from my apartment for him.

"It's supposed to get over 90 today so here, take this. I haven't even opened it yet. It's cold, straight from my fridge."

"Thanks."

Our first words to each other. I felt that blooming connection between us again. A bond growing. I think he felt it, too.

But even with that binding thread, that zing of recognition, he never spoke to me again. He never held out his hand. He never even looked at me for more than a handful of seconds. And I rarely saw him trying to make eye contact with anybody else. I think he was just for me. An insane thought, but one I had. He was my boy.

But, realistically, I knew he wasn't mine. I knew, because my boy wasn't always in the alley. And when he wasn't there, it would bother me. He left me. Where did he go? Where was his family? Did he panhandle for them? Or was he truly homeless?

You probably think I should have called someone, or taken him in myself. First of all, I did call someone. They could never find him. He was avoiding authority, they told me. He was hiding. He didn't want to go home or be put in foster care. Whatever waited for him at the end of official processing - he didn't want it. And he was clever, so he hid.

To your second point - I couldn't take him in. I had a one bedroom apartment, and my friends frequently slept over on my couch. It was no place for a child.

And finally, you probably think I should have given him more money. Believe me, I wanted to. I didn't have it. Why do you think I couldn't pay Amanda for the Miami bar tab? I had enough to live on, cloth myself, eat, get coffee, go to the gym, gas, and make my car payments. That's all my parents agreed to pay for. If I was getting a discretionary fund like Amanda, I *would* have given him more. I would have. But I was broke. So what could I do?

Classes started in September and the weather turned bitter again. My boy had been in the alley for six months now. I'd finally paid Amanda back a few weeks before. I didn't have to use the alley, anymore, but I did. Because it was something we shared. And someone had to put coins in his cup.

The autumn days grew colder and colder. The wind was starting to slip between the buildings and dumpsters and tear through my boy, trying to rip him away from me just like those train tickets back in March. It caused him to shake and shudder. Then a thunderstorm came. It lasted two days, and my boy didn't spend them in the alley. I don't know where he went. After the storm, things got even colder in the city.

Around this time, the boy and I began to make eye contact more often and for longer periods. We started to share knowing looks. His clothing was threadbare. His scraps of blanket were inconsequential to the dropping degrees. We looked at each sadly. We both knew what was coming. He wouldn't survive the winter. And when our eyes met, we agreed about that.

I brought him blankets. You know I did. I even skipped getting coffee for three days so I could bring him hot cocoa.

He used it to warm his hands but he never drank it. So I started bringing him hot water instead. And croissants. And sometimes those little cake pops. He never ate any of it, but it made me feel better that he had it.

I started leaving the back door to my apartment propped open, just a little, just in case he wanted to come inside and get warm. He watched me the first time I did it.

"You can come inside whenever you want. Sit on the stairs. It's warmer in here."

He stared at me, but he never responded. We shared a deep connection, a recognition. We spoke to each other with our eyes. Until we didn't.

I don't think he ever did come inside to get warm.

In the beginning of November, my boy stopped making eye contact with me entirely. It broke my heart. I still put quarters in his cup, but he never looked up from his mismatched shoes. Never spoke to me, or acknowledged me at all.

He started sleeping more. I would see him two days in a row and the quarters from yesterday would still be in his cup. And then he stopped leaving the alley entirely. He was there every time I looked for him, even at night. Maybe he was too cold to travel, maybe he had no where to go. Or maybe, he just wanted to be close to me.

So, I gave him more blankets. Thick ones.

Then it snowed. And it snowed again. And again. The temperature plummeted even more. But he was still there.

Bundled up in my blankets. Not making eye contact, not spending the money I gave him. Maybe he knew it was hopeless. Maybe he knew there was a date circled on some celestial calendar that said "the boy freezes to death today". We both knew it was coming.

I started bringing him hot cocoa again. But he stopped reaching for it.

The circled date ended up being the 11th of December, a Thursday. I checked on him before class. Brought him hot cocoa and adjusted his blanket tighter around his shoulders. He wasn't shaking even though it was freezing. I thought that was a good sign. I smiled at him as I left for my film noir class but he just looked away from me. I frowned. Was our connection slipping?

The day itself was bright and sunny for December. It didn't snow. I wasn't worried about him. Because it was such a nice day, I agreed to go out drinking with my friends from AP Soc. Amanda was there, having forgiven me for the delay in paying her back, and the damage to the rental car from that trip.

We tied it on, tight. I was dressed in a cute green and white striped skirt and a red sweater. It was festive and I was repping my Christmas spirit. It really wasn't a warm enough outfit for the time of year, but I'd driven my car so I wouldn't have to walk home in the cold. Plus, it looked hella cute. I hardly paid for any drinks that night.

Between the shots, and the dancing, and the body heat, I was warm. Hot even. I spun, I gyrated, I flirted, and, when it got too hot, I dipped outside for a few minutes to sneak a cigarette with Amanda and a random guy.

It was freezing. I could feel it deep in my bones immediately. The sunny day had turned into a blisteringly cold evening. As I shivered out behind the bar and sucked down that cigarette - menthol, my least favorite - I remembered my boy. And I began to worry about him.

I gave Amanda and the rest of AP Soc a bullshit excuse to leave. I needed to check on him. She made fun of me, just like she did in Miami, and I gave her the finger. I couldn't afford to be polite and drink the drinks I didn't want this time. I had to see him. Make sure he was okay.

I got my car from the valet, stiffing them on a tip. Those precious few dollars in my clutch were for my boy. I found street parking easily. It was still relatively early and everyone was out. I knocked into a garbage can as I pulled in but there was no rental company to get mad this time.

I didn't know it right away when I turned down our alley. Yeah, it was ours now. The boy's and mine. It was our alley, but I didn't notice I was alone in it. Not at first.

He was huddled into himself as always, but there was something about him that was different. His face was not buried in his jacket. It was looking across the alley, at my building's back door, the one I always used. The one I usually propped open for him. The one I hadn't, that night. I'd been too excited for my night out.

I dropped onto my knees next to him, hissing from the coldness of the ice on the bare skin of my legs.

I stared at my boy and, for the first time since I'd noticed him all those months ago, I thought he was beautiful. Absolutely stunning, actually. His greasy hair was now clean - sanitized by the intense freeze blanketing the city. And he didn't smell, not at all; the cold air was too thin to hold the heavy odors that had drifted around him through summer and autumn.

I reached out to touch him. His skin felt smooth. So smooth I sat down against the wall next to my boy so I could reach him better. I leaned against the brick and ran my numb fingers over the smoothness of his cheek. It was hard. Like marble. As if his alabaster face had been lovingly carved from a solid block of priceless stone. Carved by a master.

Yes, he was beautiful, but it was his eyes that got me. He was looking up, across the alley at the back door, his expression defiant. As if he knew today was the end, and he faced it, his head raised, tilted back, proud. Or, perhaps, he had just been waiting for me to come through that door. And I never had.

My frozen boy was dead. And there was no blood, or broken bones. No face twisted in agony.

The cold air settled around us, quiet and still, protecting and preserving his beautiful end. And it *was* beautiful. And tragic. I don't think you can have beauty without tragedy. Every story needs both. And this was ours, his and mine. But I wasn't sad. I'd always known he was familiar to me. We were connected. Always.

I dropped my hand from my frozen boy's face and leaned my head against his shoulder, cuddling up to his stiff body. And I stared at the door, like he did. His clothes weren't comfortable to lean against. The were hard. Crisp.

I stayed with him there in that alley, just my frozen boy and me. As his body grew more rigid, I began to cry, lamenting his circled date on that celestial calendar. Lamenting that it was *this* day. My boy hadn't been able to rescue himself from this end. And I hadn't been able to either.

The longer we sat, the stiffer he got, and the warmer I became. Eventually, I stopped shivering, which was nice. I cuddled into him tighter. And then, I started to feel a comfortable warmth, like a blanket wrapped around you straight out of the dryer. It was relaxing.

But the air around us started to get hotter as the hours ticked by. At first, it was a comfortable heat...and then it burned. It burned so bad, I peeled off my jacket, and then tucked back into my boy. He was still stiff.

As light finally began to streak through the mottled gray clouds above us, the air became *scorching*. So blazing, I wanted to take my clothes off, feel cool air on my skin. But I didn't want to leave my boy, not for a moment, not even for that. And my limbs weren't responding to me, anyway. So I didn't move. I cuddled closer. I wouldn't leave him. We were connected. My boy and me. Always.

He kept looking at my door, and I kept feeling stiffer. I looked at it, too, only I suddenly couldn't remember *why* we were looking at the door or who we were waiting for to come through it. I forgot why I was so hot. I forgot why I was so cold. I couldn't remember where I was, only that it was familiar to me. I knew only that I was supposed to sit here with this boy. That we were in this together, him and I. I just forgot why.

One thing I finally did remember, though, was how I knew him. This boy - he had always been familiar to me. He was there, that night in Miami. I skipped out on the bar tab. I stiffed the valet. I drove home, tired. And drunk. I hit a little boy on a deserted street and I didn't stop. He was dead. I knew he was, and I was scared. So, I kept driving. But I saw him. It was this boy, the dead one sitting next to me.

But now he wasn't there. No one was sitting next to me. I was alone in the alley, in the cold. I always had been.

I felt my brain start to panic, but then I forgot why I was upset. I forgot everything, except the door. And when the light from a cold and distant sun finally made it into the dark depths of our filthy alley...I was frozen and beautiful, too.

My Pet Monster

There hadn't *always* been monsters in the basement. That was new. Lily and Clay didn't find them right away. The young siblings had begged their Mommy for a puppy every- day for weeks. She always said no. And then the monsters appeared, like magic.

Lily remembered that day well. With no puppy to play with, she and her brother Clay had been headed down the basement steps to play with a box of old toys they sometimes took out when they were bored.

They were halfway down, just below the landing when Lily had spotted the first one. It was sitting in the corner of the room, still as stone, watching her. No, not watching, *staring,* with bulbous eyes that leaked brown fluid, like it was crying. Its mouth was open, too. It looked hungry.

Lily screamed and ran up a few stairs. Clay didn't follow. He asked what was wrong with her and she pointed at the creature with her flashlight. Her brother was a whole year older than her but Clay still screamed when he saw it. They ran.

When Mommy came home that night, they begged her to call Daddy and make him come home from his trip so he could kill the monster in the basement. Lily didn't think she believed them.

They avoided the basement and the monster living there until it rained. Mommy never played with them anymore and Daddy was still away. Clay suggested that they sneak down the stairs, get the box of toys, and run.

The first thing Lily saw when she got to the landing was that the monster was still there, guarding the box. It looked angrier. Meaner. Its mouth was wider, it looked hungrier. Starving. And it watched them.

Clay was much braver than her. He got on the floor and crawled toward the box. He was smart. The monster didn't glance toward him, maybe it didn't even see him. It just kept looking at her. Staring, mocking. She knew it wanted her to come down off the steps. But she wouldn't.

She pointed the flashlight toward the monster in the corner, hoping the light would blind it. She didn't want it to look at her anymore. Movement from the other side of the box made Lily swing the flashlight away from the creature. She swept the light over and she saw it.

Two monsters. This one was watching Clay intently. No surprise because Clay was *touch- ing it,* like he couldn't help himself.

"Don't! It's gonna bite you, Clay!"

"It wouldn't bite me, its teeth are too small."

Clay stuck his finger in its mouth and Lily screamed. The creature watched him do it, but didn't bite down. Clay scraped his finger across its little teeth and when his finger came away, there was blood on it.

"Sharp! It cut you!" She whispered to him. "Come back. Please. I don't want the box anymore, Clay."

"Stop being a baby."

Clay wasn't interested in the box anymore, either. He petted the second creature and it didn't hurt him. Just watched him.

"Maybe they could be our pets." He said. "There's one for each of us."

"I don't want a monster as a pet!" Lily yelled.

"I wanna go back upstairs." "Then go. They can both be my pets."

Lily's eyes were drawn back to the one in the corner. It looked at her. Only ever at her. And she knew, she *knew*. That one was hers. "I wanted a dog, though." Lily whined.

Clay kept petting his monster. "You're a good boy, aren't you? Yes, you are. My finger doesn't even hurt. You wouldn't hurt your new master, would you?"

Lily watched Clay with his monster and started to feel a little bit jealous. *Daddy had been away for almost three weeks in New York and Mommy never plays with us, anymore. We're too old now. And it's raining outside.* Maybe a monster for a pet wasn't such a bad idea. Clay seemed to like his and it hadn't hurt him yet.

Lily looked over at her creature. His eyes seemed needy. He wanted her love. She knew he did. He never looked away from her.

Lily stuck her foot out and let it hang over the concrete for two dramatic seconds be- fore setting it on the floor.

"You're a good monster. Good boy. Do you want some-thing to eat? You don't have to eat me, I can get you food."

Listening to her brother try to bond with his creature-pet gave her courage. Lily ran over to her monster and dropped down in front of him. He just watched her. She brushed a little, shaking finger along his face, avoiding his teeth, which were long. The monster's mouth remained open but he didn't snap at her.

"Oooooh, you're so cute. I can feed you. What do you like to eat?" She cooed to it. "Mine stinks. Does yours smell bad, too?" Clay asked.

She leaned in, making sure to keep far away from his teeth in case her pet was *really* hungry. "Yes, he smells. I think they need bathes. Poor things.

"They're monsters, stupid, we're not gonna give 'em a bath. Let's find them some food to eat."

"Mine has gray skin," Lily said, looking him over. She pet his head and looked back at her brother. "Do you think they're aliens?"

"I don't know, maybe." Clay said. "What color is yours?"

"Mine is like purple, sort of."

She laughed. "Are you sure yours isn't a girl?"

"He's not a girl! Yours is a girl!"

"Maybe," she nodded. "It's a little smaller than yours."

SCRAPE

Clay bolted to his feet and looked at the ceiling above them.

"Mom is home. Come on, let's go."

"But these poor babies need something to eat!" Lily objected.

"We'll bring them something tonight, after Mom's asleep." He answered. "We can't let her find them. She won't understand they're nice, she'll just kill them or call the police and they'll be taken to a lab."

"What's a lab?"

"A place where people take weird things."

"They wouldn't be nice to them there?"

"No! They'd hurt them."

Lily threw her arms around her new pet. "No! I won't let anyone hurt Daisy!" As if to agree, Daisy's head tipped and nuzzled Lily's arm.

"You're naming yours Daisy?"

"Yes. Just because she's an ugly monster doesn't mean she doesn't deserve a pretty name."

"So yours *is* a girl?" He asked.

"Yes, I think she is." Lily said, petting the creature's head and back. Daisy's skin was hard, it felt unbreakable. *I bet she could protect me really well in a fight.*

"Mine's name is...Brick."

"Brick?" Lily wrinkled her nose. "What kind of a name is Brick?"

Clay stopped petting his monster and tried to lift him off the ground. Brick was too heavy and Clay had to drop him. The monster didn't attack, though, and Clay went back to petting him. "See? He weighs as much as a pile of bricks."

"Mine has hard skin. Can we sneak back down and feed them later?"

"Yeah. After Mom's asleep. She can never know about them."

"I don't want her to hurt them! I don't care what they are. They're ours!"

They each gave their pets one more soothing stroke and then Lily kissed Daisy's head and crept back upstairs. That night, long after Mommy had fallen asleep, Clay and Lily snuck back into the basement loaded with poptarts and raw chicken.

And though they tried hard, they couldn't get their pets to eat either. Clay was frustrated and told her they should try bugs the next day. After a few more pets and cuddles, the kids snuck back up to their room.

The light around the windows was turned from gray to pink when they finally got back into bed.

"Clay..." Lily said right before she closed her eyes. She knew Mom should be waking them soon but she didn't regret staying up to bond with Daisy. Not one bit.

"Yeah?" He said from under the covers of his bed.

"I don't want Mommy to kill the monsters. I like Daisy and Brick. What if she finds them?"

"Mom doesn't go down into the basement anymore. She wont find them."

"But-"

"Besides, I was thinking maybe we could train them. To protect us."

"From Mommy?"

But Clay didn't answer. He was asleep.

Mommy didn't find out about their pets. They continued trying to feed Daisy and Brick, but the creatures didn't like anything the siblings gave them. Lily was frustrated. Daisy's mouth kept getting wider and wider, until she looked really scary. But she still wouldn't eat.

And Brick, all he got was bigger - everywhere. Bigger and bloated, almost twice as big as he was before. Clay couldn't even wrap his arms around Brick.

But their pets never hurt them. Never bit, hit, or attacked. Lily and Clay played with them everyday. They took care of their pets, were responsible. Bathed them when they smelled too bad, dressed them up, cared for them. Bonded with them. *If only Mommy could see how responsible we are with our pets,* Lily thought, *she would finally let us get a dog.*

But Mommy still ignored them. So Lily and Clay gave up behaving and simply moved into the basement to be with Daisy and Brick. They weren't comfy to cuddle with, but at least Lily didn't feel so alone. Everything was wonderful. And Mommy never said a word about it.

Until Daddy came home.

They were in the basement playing with their pets the day Daddy finally came back from his long trip. Clay put a finger to his lips and Lily listened to Daddy giving Mommy a kiss hello and then ask where they were. She didn't answer, probably because she didn't know. She never paid attention. He asked again and Lily could hear Mommy mumble something to him. She hugged Daisy tightly. If Daddy came down and found Daisy and Brick he would hurt them. He wouldn't see that they were nice, just that they were monsters.

"Where are the kids, Helen?" Daddy asked again.

"The basement." She replied, so quiet.

Lily's panicked eyes found Clay. "They'll find them!" Clay started crying, trying to drag Brick, who was too big and heavy now, into a dark corner. Lily just held onto Daisy and sobbed.

Daddy opened the door. "Kids?"

"Don't come down here, Daddy!" Lily yelled. He went down a few steps.

"Clay? Lily?"

"No, Daddy, don't!" She screamed.

But Daddy kept coming. He reached the bottom stair and pulled the light string, the one Clay and her weren't tall enough to reach.

"Oh my God, Helen. What have you done?"

Mommy was behind him on the stairs, looking down with dull eyes. Glazed over blue eyes, sort of like Daisy's. Mommy also had long, blonde hair, just like Daisy's. *Like mine, too,* Lily thought.

"They wouldn't stop bothering me, Richard. Snacks, entertainment, they wanted a dog. A goddamn dog! They wouldn't stop! Everyday, it was like torture! I couldn't take it!"

She didn't cry, but Daddy did. He ran over next to Lily and fell down, then hugged Daisy and started rocking her.

"Daddy, that's my pet," Lily whispered, confused.

But Daddy yelled. "Helen, what did you do? What did you do, you fucking bitch?!" Lily's eyes widened and she looked over at Clay, shocked Daddy had sworn in front of them. Clay's eyes seemed sad. Like he understood something.

"Why did you say that word in front of us, Daddy?" Lily asked.

"Lily... Oh my God, my kids." He said.

"I'm right here, Daddy." Lily said. But he ignored her, too, just like Mommy. "What's wrong with them, Clay?" Lily whispered.

Clay looked sad, like he didn't want to tell her.

"What's happening?" She asked him again. "Are they gonna kill Daisy and Brick?"

"No." He said.

"Why no?" She asked, but maybe she knew.

"'Cause, Lily...Mommy already killed the monsters in the basement. They're..." Clay didn't finish.

But she understood.

LAKE WILCOM

The lake has been frozen over since October. I know that because I was here when the ice formed. I've had this cabin for about a decade but I usually only stay a few weeks when I need some distance from the world. No one lives on Lake Wilcom but me. I built this cabin in my 30's and then bought a 4-wheeler so I could get back here in the summer.

Unfortunately, the snowfall was early this year. I can't get out and I know I'm probably stuck here until spring. It's no problem, really, I'm self employed and the cabin is well stocked. And it's just me to worry about. I'll get more solitude than I intended but that's okay, too. Plenty of books and whiskey in my cabin.

This morning started like all the other mornings. I woke up, made some coffee, sat in the bay window to drink it while I watched the sunrise. But as the gray streaks in the sky lightened to muted yellow, I noticed a shape out on the ice of Lake Wilcom. The object slowly gained definition over the next 30 minutes and I kept watching, confused.

There was no one out here. No town for miles and miles. No roads to get back here. That's why I built here. But there it was in the middle of the frozen lake - a fucking pram.

My coffee went cold as I studied it, contemplated it. Who was out here? Why did they leave a baby buggy in the middle of the lake? Was it a joke? Was it empty? God, I hoped it was empty.

I finally left the bay window but checked on the black baby carriage throughout the day. I wondered if I should go out there and see if anything was inside of it. But I didn't know much about frozen lakes and how much weight they could support. I'm a big man. What if I fell through? And the buggy had been out there all night. If there was anything in it, it was already dead. But still, someone had to push it out there and leave it. Why? My cabin was visible from the middle of the lake. Was someone fucking with me?

There were days I forgot about the pram entirely and days I couldn't stop staring at it. The carriage froze, then thawed. Then froze again. One morning I woke up to a snow storm so bad it had completely buried the pram in snow. But I saw the lump in the middle of the lake. I knew it was still there.

It was early March when the weather finally broke. The access road to the cabin became drivable again but I didn't leave. I wanted to wait for the snow to melt more. I wanted to see the baby buggy one last time before I left Lake Wilcom. Wanted to make sure it hadn't been a hallucination brought on by extreme isolation.

It wasn't until the middle of April that the snow melted enough that I could see the baby carriage again. The shade over the top of the cradle was torn and weathered. It whipped around in the early spring winds. Something else flapped there too, a baby blanket that hung out from the inside. It thrashed around angrily but never escaped the pram. As if it was weighted down.

I packed that night, ready to leave Lake Wilcom. For so many months it had just been me and that baby carriage. I was ready to drown in the big world once more.

When the sun rose on Easter morning I pulled on a sweatshirt and parka then loaded the car with my things. I took inventory of the cabin and made a list of supplies I would need to restock it after being stuck at the lake for an entire winter. Before I departed, I went to take one last look at the baby carriage.

But it was gone. All I could see where it had once sat for so many months was broken ice and glistening blue lake water. I left and didn't return for two years.

I came back to Lake Wilcom in August of 2012. Before hitting the cabin I stopped in a nearby town called Brire to pick up the supplies that needed replacing from that winter a couple of years before. While I was there, I had lunch and read the local paper. It wasn't on the front page, or even the second. The article was buried in the back, in the "Local News" section.

Brire Family Not Giving Up Hope for Return of Baby Benjamin

I didn't read the article, because I didn't have to. Below the headline was a picture of an attractive middle aged couple holding a baby. Behind them, a black pram with a blue blanket inside. I'd seen that baby carriage in my dreams off and on. It was the one from the lake, I was sure.

I left the cafe and headed up to Lake Wilcom. It was late afternoon by the time I got there. Everything was as I left it inside. I walked to the bay window and looked out at the lake. It shimmered before me, welcoming; beautiful blue waves reflecting an orange and pink sky.

I watched the sunset. I grilled a T-Bone. I read a book. I left the next morning.

Because as hard as I tried, I couldn't stop myself from returning to the window time and time again. I couldn't help but stare out of it, my eyes drawn to the place where the buggy used to be.

I couldn't forget what was at the bottom of the lake. Knowledge I shared with only one other person who was out there somewhere.

I put my cabin on the market the following year. No one bought it, perhaps because of its isolation and accessibility. I took it off the market last year, but I'll never return. The lake belongs to someone else now.

So the cabin sits alone on the shores of Lake Wilcom year after year. Winter after winter. Summer after summer. And the lake is quiet and smooth. Still and calm. Alone and forsaken. It's been that way for years and it'll be that way for years more. Just the lake, my cabin, and Baby Benjamin.

GRAY

Alice (AP reporter): "May I record this interview Melanie?"

Melanie: "I suppose."

Click.

Alice (AP reporter): "Alright. Today is February 19th, 2058 and I am in Brainard, Minnesota interviewing Melanie Haggens of the failed Starburst Mission."

Melanie: *Clears throat.* "It's Richards now."

Alice (AP reporter): "I'm sorry?"

Melanie: *A little louder.* "My last name is Richards now."

Alice (AP reporter): "Oh, of course. My apologies. Mrs. Richards, you have been missing since the return of the Starburst mission and it was only with great effort and expense that I was able to track you down almost a decade later. Is it true that you were hidden by the government after your team returned from Mars?"

Melanie: "No, not by the government. By the others."

Alice (AP reporter): "The others?"

Melanie: "The others on the mission."

Alice (AP reporter): "I see. And were you aware there is renewed interest in your case? In the events that took place during your time on Mars?"

Melanie: "No. Why is there renewed interest? I think we all just want to forget about what happened. It was so long ago."

Alice (AP reporter): "It was actually less than a decade ago. Mrs. Richards, were you debriefed when you returned from the Starburst mission?"

Melanie: "No. Actually, I- I haven't spoken of it in 9 years."

Alice (AP reporter): "Since you returned in 2049."

Melanie: "That's right. I was sent here to Brainard. I met Ted here."

Alice (AP reporter): "Your husband?"

Melanie: "Yes. Why is there suddenly interest in Starburst again?"

Alice (AP reporter): "And you haven't spoken about the events that took place on Deco Base with your husband?"

Melanie: "Of course not. I'm a different person now. I work at the library now. And my name is Kristen Richards."

Alice (AP reporter): "But you *are* Melanie Haggens, the botanist on the 2041 Starburst mission to Mars, correct?"

Melanie: "I used to be."

Alice (AP reporter): "Your husband doesn't know you were an astronaut?"

Melanie: "No. He…"

Alice (AP reporter): "He what?"

Melanie: "He wouldn't believe me anyway."

Alice (AP reporter): "Why not?"

Melanie: "Because of Gray."

Alice (AP reporter): "I'm sorry, who is Gray?"

Melanie: "She's…a little girl."

Alice (AP reporter): "I'm confused, Mrs. Richards."

Pause.

Melanie: "What do you want to know about the Starburst mission?"

Alice (AP reporter): "Right... Melanie, let's start at the beginning. Interviews have been published with all seven other members of Starburst and every single one of them has refused to speak abut what happened during your eight years on Deco Base."

Melanie: "Yes. I- I wouldn't think they would want to talk about it."

Alice (AP reporter): "The government has even threatened a few of them with prison time but no one will admit how the seven of you escaped Deco Base after the marsquake. You have never been formally or informally interviewed because no one could find you. Would you like to talk about the events at Deco Base, now?"

Pause.

Alice (AP reporter): "Melanie?"

Melanie: "I…"

Alice (AP reporter): "Are you alright? What are you looking at?"

Young child's voice: "She's looking at Gray."

Alice (AP reporter): "Oh, hello."

Young child's voice: "My name's Teagan. Are you interviewing Mommy for TV?"

Alice (AP reporter): "I'm interviewing your mommy for an article."

Young child's voice: "Oh. Well you can't interview Gray. She doesn't talk."

Alice (AP reporter): "And who is Gray?"

Melanie: "Teagan, go to your room now."

Young child's voice: "But-"

Melanie: "Go!"

Teagan leaves.

Melanie: "I'm sorry about that."

Alice (AP reporter): "Melanie... would you like to talk about Gray?"

Melanie: "Oh, Gray is just my kids' imaginary friend. That's - that's what my husband says."

Alice (AP reporter): "I see. And what do you say?"

Melanie: "Teagan starting talking about her as soon as he could complete sentences. He describes her as short, blonde. Maybe 5 or 6 years old. She..."

Alice (AP reporter): "She what?"

Melanie: "She always has her head tilted to the side. On her shoulder, like this. They say she

has one arm raised high in the air over her head. Her little fingers gripping something."

Alice (AP reporter): "They?"

Melanie: "Both of my children claim they see Gray."

Alice (AP reporter): "Does she speak to them?"

Melanie: "No. She cannot talk. She only stares."

Alice (AP reporter): "Alright. Melanie, do you see her, too?"

Melanie: "Yes. My husband doesn't believe me."

Alice (AP reporter): "Is Gray here right now?"

Melanie: "She's always here."

Alice (AP reporter): "I see. Melanie, have you spoken to a doctor about Gray?"

Melanie: "No. A doctor can't help Gray."

Alice (AP reporter): "Alright. Well...let's return to Starburst. You were only 24 when you were offered a place on the mission, correct?"

Melanie: "Starburst...yes. I had just graduated. My final year I had a paper published-"

Alice (AP reporter): "The Solar Effort theory."

Melanie: "Yes. The IMC thought it was brilliant. They wanted me to test out my theories on Mars. They told me all about Deco Base, which was almost completed at that time. We actually passed Journey 1 on our way to Mars."

Alice (AP reporter): "Were you very excited?"

Melanie: "Yes. I was so young and...idealistic. I was certain I could grow vegetable bearing plants in Mars soil in a controlled environment, such as on Deco Base."

Alice (AP reporter): "So you left in 2040 with your seven other crew members: four other scientists, a pilot, a medic, and a technical expert."

Melanie: "Yes. I was the youngest but...they were all very nice to me. Cragson especially was interested in my research."

Alice (AP reporter): "Mitch Cragson. The geneticist."

Melanie: "Yes, Mitch."

Alice (AP reporter): "Did you get along with everyone?"

Melanie: "Bonham, the pilot. She and I were close."

Alice (AP reporter): "What about Andrew Belker?" *Pause.*

Melanie: "I don't want to talk about Andrew."

Alice (AP reporter): "Alright. But you got along with everyone?"

Melanie: "More or less... They were all older than me. In their 30s and 40s. It was hard at first."

Alice (AP reporter): "I'd imagine so. So you arrived in January of 2041. What was that like?"

Melanie: "It was nice to get off the ship. Everyone had driven each other a bit crazy by then. Cabin fever and all that."

Alice (AP reporter): "Tell me about Deco Base."

Melanie: "It was...big. Not that big thinking back but compared to the Journey 2 it was massive. I only had to share my room with one other person."

Alice (AP reporter): "Amanda Clark."

Melanie: "Yes, Clark. She didn't like me much."

Alice (AP reporter): "She was in a relationship with Andrew Belker, is that right?"

Melanie: "I said I don't want to talk about Andrew."

Alice (AP reporter): "Of course. I'm sorry. Now, you were meant to remain at Deco Base for 13 months before returning to earth, correct?"

Melanie: "Yes."

Alice (AP reporter): "And when did the marsquake happen?"

Melanie: "May. Only four months into the mission."

Alice (AP reporter): "Can you tell me about what happened that day?"

Melanie: "Everyone was in the Lab. It was the main room, the largest room of Deco Base. Mitch, he- he noticed one of tomatoes I had grown was a sort of purple instead of red or yellow. He wanted to document this and returned to his room for his laptop. He hadn't been gone more than 2 minutes or so when it happened. I'm from California so I knew what it was right away. Everything just...shook. I could hear things crashing and falling. I hid under a table. Everyone else did, too. It lasted four minutes maybe. Afterward so much was broken. A lot of our equipment. The tunnels. The staging door."

Alice (AP reporter): "And Mitch Cragson?"

Melanie: "He was trapped in his room. The tunnels had collapsed. None of them were compromised but they were impassable. We couldn't get to him or he to us. Oxygen was still flowing to the lab but...we don't know if it reached the rooms. I hope not. It's better that Mitch just fell asleep then...then starved to death."

Alice (AP reporter): "Of course. I understand. Melanie, tell me about the next few minutes after the quake?"

Melanie: "Everyone was in shock. Then mad, at Clark. They thought since she was the geologist she should have anticipated the marsquake. She said that it was impossible to predict. She said it isn't like earth and it should only happen once every million years or so. There was a lot of fighting and arguing. I didn't say anything. I was scared."

Alice (AP reporter): "You were only 24."

Melanie: "25 by then. I'd had a birthday at Deco Base."

Alice (AP reporter): "So what happened over the next few days?"

Melanie: "We inventoried everything. What equipment had survived and what was broken. We talked a lot about what to do. Should we finish the mission and leave in February as planned or depart for earth immediately? Technically we had enough food to last, and even if we didn't we could grow it. Most of the equipment we needed to continue our research had survived. But... we were all stuck in one room together. Everyone had turned on Amanda Clark, even Andrew. Everyone was mad at her. Everyone was miserable. Our Communication Scatter was wrecked.

There would be no further contact with San Diego until we could get in range of Earth on the Journey 2, which, we weren't even sure if the craft had survived."

Alice (AP reporter): "So what happened?"

Melanie: "In the end we decided to return home immediately."

Alice (AP reporter): "Everyone agreed?"

Melanie: "All of us, unanimously. It was horrible, all living in one room together. One toilet, two sinks, no shower. So we all suited up, and went to leave Deco Base."

Alice (AP reporter): "Alright, Melanie, most of what you've told me so far has been public knowledge. Everything that happened next has never been spoken of by the Starburst team so I'd like you to give as much detail about the following events as possible."

Melanie: "Alright, well..."

Pause.

Alice (AP reporter): "Melanie?"

Pause.

Alice (AP reporter): "Melanie? Mrs. Richards? What are you looking at?"

Pause.

Alice (AP reporter): Is it the little girl, again?

Melanie: "I need to finish telling you. Everything."

Alice (AP reporter): "Would you like a glass of water?"

Melanie: "No. I'm fine."

Alice (AP reporter): "Melanie...does Gray have anything to do with what happened at Deco Base?"

Melanie: *Quietly.* "We didn't know she was there."

Alice (AP reporter): "Wait. Are you saying there was a child at Deco Base? Melanie, please concentrate. The mission before Starburst was Element. Element built Deco Base, you said you passed their ship on the way. Are you telling me, on record, that they left behind a child?"

Melanie: "Please just let me finish telling you everything. We-we *did* know she was there. But...please don't judge us. We didn't know what else to do."

Alice (AP reporter): "There were reports of a pregnancy on the Element Mission but the official summary said the pregnancy was terminated."

Melanie: "You don't understand the state our minds were in at the time."

Alice (AP reporter): "Tell me about the child, Melanie."

Melanie: "You have to understand the rest first. It...the door was two phase. A lever on the security console opened the door to the staging bay, where our suits were. It used a biometric human heat signature to authorize the egress sequence. The lever, when you pulled it, would start a 30 second countdown to let everyone get inside the staging bay. There were a further four minutes to put on our suits before the lab door closed and the door to the atmosphere opened. It took approximately one minute to don the suit and the sequence could be aborted at anytime from inside the staging bay."

Alice (AP reporter): "And this is what the remaining seven of you attempted."

Melanie: "Yes. But the system had been broken. When we tried to initiate the egress sequence, the countdown started. But immediately after you took your hand off the lever, the sequence aborted."

Alice (AP reporter): "What does that mean?"

Melanie: "It means that in order complete the sequence, and open the door, the lever could not be dropped. If it was dropped, the system aborted the egress sequence entirely."

Alice (AP reporter): "Meaning that in order to open the door to the atmosphere, someone had to remain behind and hold the lever."

Melanie: "Exactly."

Alice (AP reporter): "My God. So someone needed to sacrifice themselves in order for the rest of you to escape."

Melanie: "Yes. And wait for those of us who had escaped to contact mission control in San Diego. Then San Diego would need to scramble a mission to rescue the remaining person. That would take a year or so, even if everything moved at a breakneck pace."

Alice (AP reporter): "And no one offered to stay behind?"

Melanie: "Not even one of us. We knew...well, the IMC was not well funded under the administration we left when we departed earth. We talked about it quite a bit. We all knew there was a fair chance that the IMC would not see the cost benefit in sending a rescue mission for one person after a failed mission. They had just dumped billions into Riso Base on the other side of the planet."

Alice (AP reporter): "Couldn't six of you escape and then open the door from the outside to let the remaining person out?"

Melanie: "No. That sequence was also part of the damaged console."

Alice (AP reporter): "And your technical expert tried to repair it?"

Melanie: "Yes. Belker, he...he said it was all broken."

Alice (AP reporter): "I see. So the only option was for someone to stay behind and pray help would be sent."

Melanie: "Yes."

Alice (AP reporter): "Melanie, all seven of you came back."

Melanie: *Quietly* "Yes."

Alice (AP reporter): "How?"

Melanie: "Because of her."

Alice (AP reporter): "The child left behind by the Element mission?"

Melanie: "Because of- of Gray."

Pause.

Melanie: "She was...she didn't talk. She didn't have any facial expressions or personality. It wasn't like she was even a human being."

Alice (AP reporter): "Melanie, I know Deco Base was large, but how had a child hidden there for so many months? Survived so many months alone and then hidden from your team when you arrived on Deco Base?"

Melanie: "You don't understand. She wasn't really a *person*."

Alice (AP reporter): "Can you explain that?"

Melanie: "No one ever interacted with her. She was used to being alone or..or ignored I think."

Alice (AP reporter): "Melanie, this is very important...did you use the child you discovered on Deco Base to hold the lever so that seven of you could escape?"

Melanie: "We had to."

Alice (AP reporter): *Angry.* "You left a child there? Alone?"

Melanie: "There was plenty of food. The tomatoes were growing, potatoes, even cabbage-"

Alice (AP reporter): *Horrified.* "She was a child, Mrs. Richards!"

Melanie: "She wasn't. But, she could feed herself. And water."

Alice (AP reporter): "And after you left, you never let anyone know? Organized rescue for her?"

Melanie: "We couldn't. We knew we couldn't, we talked about it. Everyone would know what we'd done."

Alice (AP reporter): "Your team is disgusting. Despicable. But even so, she could still be saved. It's been nine years since you've returned. If what you said is true, Gray could still be alive."

Melanie: "No. No, she's dead. The crops would have gone through their natural life cycle. There would be no food after five years or so..."

Pause.

Alice (AP reporter): "No. I can't... Holy mother of God. If true, this is a monstrous act. I've never heard anything quite like it. Melanie, what you and your team did was...inhuman."

Melanie: "You don't understand. She was blank. Just a body. Just a- a- a shell! No one spoke to her for years. There was nothing there."

Alice (AP reporter): "She was a child, and you *used* her. *Sacrificed* her to survive. A little girl. Alone on a planet with no one!"

Melanic: "No. She wasn't real."

Alice (AP reporter): "She was real. If you used her to open the door, to push up the lever, the biometrics, Mrs. Richards, Gray was *very* real. I see now why she haunts your home, your mind, even your children."

Melanie: "No, you don't understand at all. She wasn't a real child. I have real children. They smile and laugh and play. Gray was simply a tool. Andrew, he reconfigured the system to recognize her. We taught her how to hold the lever up. She never asked a question. Never showed an emotion. She was more of a, a robot maybe."

Alice (AP reporter): "No, she wasn't. This is what you and the others tell yourselves to assuage the guilt about what you'd done. No wonder Starburst hid you away from the public. What you did stripped you of your humanity. All of you."

Melanie: "It was eight years. We were stuck in that fucking lab for eight years! You would have done it, too. I know you would have."

Alice (AP reporter): "Eight years, that is what doesn't make sense to me. You must have found Gray immediately. Discovered her within the first year or so. And yet it took seven more years for you to find the "courage" to do what you did."

Melanie: "You still don't understand."

Alice (AP reporter): "When this drops, Mrs. Richards, it will destroy the Starburst legacy AND that of Element. Everyone will be held responsible."

Melanie: "You're not listening! Element had nothing to do with this!"

Alice (AP reporter): "Element lied about a pregnancy termination and left a child alone on a planet for five months!"

Melanie: "She wasn't from the Element mission!"

Alice (AP reporter): "Are you saying she was a martian, Mrs. Richards?"

Melanie: "No!"

Alice (AP reporter): "A phantom!"

Melanie: "Of course not!"

Alice (AP reporter): "Then where did Gray come from?!"

Melanie: "We made her!"

Pause.

Melanie: "We made her, alright?"

Alice (AP reporter): "What are you... just what are you saying?"

Melanie: *Crying.* "We needed another person. Someone to satisfy the biometrics. Someone to hold the lever."

Alice (AP reporter): "So you..."

Melanie: "I was chosen. I was the youngest. The most fertile."

Alice (AP reporter): "My god..."

Melanie: "Andrew, he...he volunteered. It took two months. I was pregnant for eight and a half. Avenson, our medic. He delivered Gray. And then..and then we knew we had to wait. We figured when she was four, maybe five, she would be strong enough to hold the lever up."

Alice (AP reporter): "You... you made a baby. You raised it. With the sole purpose of sacrifice?"

Melanie: "We fed her but, we barely ever spoke directly to her. Never looked at her. Never touched her. Amanda hated her, I think because of what Gray was to Andrew. She was the only one who gave Gray any attention. The only time the rest of us acknowledged her was when she was old enough to understand that she had an important job. We described the lever to her. Told her everyone had a purpose and this was hers. But...she was a small child. Malnourished, we all were. She should have been able to hold the lever at 4 but she was slight and short. It took until she was 6."

Alice (AP reporter): "You are all monsters."

Melanie: "No, no, you still don't understand. *Gray* was the monster. That's why we called her Gray, her skin was Gray from lack of sunlight and poor diet. She was born without a soul. No personality. Don't you see? Because she was born to be a tool, that's all she was. A shell. There was nothing behind her eyes. If you could see her, standing there against the wall right now, you would know what I mean. You would know we weren't monsters. Gray was."

Alice (AP reporter): "She haunts you. Everyday."

Melanie: "On the day we decided we could finally trust her to hold the lever for the full four and a half minutes, we told her to do her very important job. I remember looking back through the staging bay door. I could see her, skinny, little arm high over her head holding up the lever. She stared at me as I pulled my helmet on, stared still as I turned away for the last time. See, we never told Gray where she came from but I think she knew. I think she knew I made her."

Alice (AP reporter): "And she's still standing there. Staring at you. Holding the lever, even now."

Melanie: "Even now. She stares... I worry one day, one day she will drop it."

Alice (AP reporter): "It wouldn't matter. She's a ghost of your shame and you're safely back on earth, now. The child you created to pay for that opportunity died alone on a distant planet. No one is holding that lever anymore, Melanie."

Melanie: *Quietly.* "You're wrong. I can see her right now."

Alice (AP reporter): "What you see is only a manifestation of your guilt."

Melanie: "No, no, no. There is no guilt. She wasn't a child. Do you get it? We created her for one purpose and it wasn't to be anyone's child. Do you understand?"

Alice (AP reporter): "This interview is over."

Melanie: "Tell me you understand! Tell me you know that Gray was just a purpose, not a human being! She was only the lever!"

Alice (AP reporter): "Thank you for your time, the article will post within 48 hours."

Melanie: "She wasn't a child like my Teagan or Avery! You know that right? She wasn't my child!"

Alice (AP reporter): "Goodbye, Mrs. Richards."

Melanie: "Wait! Wait. Please. Just tell me. Why do people care about Deco Base again? Why the renewed interest?"

Alice (AP reporter): "Because, Melanie, the ICM recently received a ping from the ether of space, from 33 million miles away. Right in the vicinity of Mars, actually. But no one is there. Right? Except...now we know that is a lie."

Melanie: "No, Gray is dead! She definitely dead! Whatever they're bringing back is-" *Click.*

Rocking A Ranch

It was the summer between 6th and 7th grade that we moved to Ralling, a medium sized town outside of Milwaukee. My parents bought a nice house in a nice neighborhood with a nice bit of forest behind the cul-de-sac. My little brother Jake met a kid his age while playing street hockey alone. Turned out the kid lived right next door to us.

Jake and Danny became fast friends and bogarted our pool for most of the summer. It wasn't until Danny's older brother came to collect him one day that I found out there was a kid *my* age living next door, too.

His name was Andy and he was cool as hell. We played xbox, and x-games. Danny and Jake hated it because we always kicked them out of the pool so we could ride our bikes into it playing BMX.

One weekend I brought out my skateboard and taught Andy how to skate. He was terrible, but it was fun. He never cried when he fell.

Andy always wanted to hang out and my house, never his. I wasn't really sure why so I asked Jake if there was something weird about their house, since he was allowed to go inside with Danny. Jake said no, only that Andy's bedroom door was always locked. Maybe there were dead bodies in the room. I rolled my eyes. Little kids are dumb.

Some weekends Andy couldn't play because he was off "working with his dad" who was a cop. I thought that was cool until I caught him in the lie. One day Andy went off to "work with his dad" but later I saw his dad mowing the grass while Andy was gone. When I asked Andy about it, he said he didn't want to tell me where he was. I pressed him and he left. I didn't see him for four days. Those days were very boring without Andy.

I cornered Danny during that time and demanded to know what secret thing Andy did on the weekends. Jake and Danny just snickered and ran away. They both knew, I know they did. But I decided not to push it. Andy would tell me when he was ready. But he never came over.

I finally went over to Andy's house and demanded to see him. His mother eyed me warily but took me up to Andy's room and knocked on the door. Andy answered. His face went white when he saw me. He tried to close the door so I couldn't see into his room, but I saw everything anyway.

60

Andy was really, REALLY into horses. There were posters and statues of them all over his room. The first thing out of my mouth wasn't the right thing to say.

"Do you have a sister I don't know about?"

I saw the tears in his eyes before Andy slammed the door in my face. Mrs. Barden pulled me away. "You know, Elliot, boys can like horses, too."

I felt like crying as I was led down the stairs and out the front door. My only friend in this new city was mad at me.

"I know. I'm sorry Mrs. Barden."

The next day I went back over the Andy's house. I brought with me a book about horses I'd found on our bookshelf as a peace offering. Danny and Jake with there, playing xbox in the living room.

"Have you guys seen Andy?"

They both ignored me. I threw the book at my brother. "Yo! Is Andy here?"

Danny shrugged. "Nah, he's out behind the house mining for diamonds or something."

"Diamonds?"

Danny paused the game and turned around to look at me. "Yeah, he likes gemstones and rocks and stuff."

"Bullshit. Whatever, you guys are lame." I said before turning back out the door. Something hit me square in the shoulders. I turned around to see that Jake had thrown the book back at me.

"Don't fucking throw stuff at me, Eli!"

"I'm telling Dad you swore," I said, picking the book up off the ground.

Jake was up and pulling on my arm before I'd even straightened. "No, you can't. He'll get mad and hit me."

I laughed. "Dad would *not* hit you."

"Please, Eli, *please* don't tell Dad. I cry when he yells at me and he laughs and says I'm not being a man because I cry."

"Oh my god, fine, get off me." I shrugged him away and left out the front door slamming it behind me.

I found Andy pretty deep in the woods behind his house. He was digging in the dirt near a creek bed and had a neat stack of rocks next to him. He didn't bother to look at me as I approached.

"You gonna make fun of my minerals, too?"

I sat down and inspected the pile stacked carefully beside him. "No. I didn't mean to make fun of you yesterday either. I think it's cool you're into horses."

"You know cowboys are into horses. There's nothing girly about them."

"I know, man, I'm sorry. The posters took me off guard. Horses are cool. I rode one once at the fair."

Andy nodded, still not looking at me. "Yeah. I ride every other weekend."

So that's where he went on the weekends. "That's cool. I would have gone with you. It's boring when you're gone."

"You would have laughed at me."

"No, I wouldn't!"

"You would've. I'm the only boy in riding class."

I didn't know what to say to that so I slid the book over to him across the dirt. He eyed it before hesitantly picking it up.

"*Loving the Duke of Horseflesh?*"

"Yeah. It's a book about horses. There's a horse on the cover."

"Who's the *guy* on the cover?"

"I dunno. Horse trainer?"

"He's pretty jacked."

"Yeah, horse trainers get lots of exercise, right?"

Andy shrugged."Yeah, I guess they do."

A train blew its horn in the distance. I always loved when the trains went by. I could feel the ground below me hum and bristle as 6000 tons of grinding machine thundered over it a quarter mile away. Andy continued to dig and we let the silence settle again. It was almost a full minute before Andy broke it.

"I like rocks. Different kinds of rocks. See this? This is agate and this is quartz."

I nodded. "I've heard of quartz."

"I've been looking for malachite forever. It's green

"That's cool."

There was silence again broken only by the creek bubbling nearby. I tried to think of something to say but I knew nothing about rocks.

"The kids at school make fun of me."

"About the rocks?"

Andy nodded. "Mostly about horses. But sometimes about the minerals, too."

"That's dumb. I'll bet they're into weird stuff, too.

"Horse aren't weird!"

"No, that's not what-"

"And neither are minerals! I'm gonna have a ranch one day in Wyoming and I'm gonna breed horses and mine for precious metals and gemstones. I'm gonna call it *Rocking A Ranch.*

Because there's horse and rocks and it'll be *mine*. I'll be rich and everyone will want to come to my ranch and I won't let them."

"You won't let me come?"

Andy dug into the dirt with his spade, refusing to look at me. "I don't know."

"Look, I'm sorry, okay? I think it's cool you're into this stuff."

"Whatever."

"You wanna know something embarrassing that I'm into?"

"You don't have to tell me."

"Well, you told me so it's only fair. I like baking."

"Baking?"

"I do it with my mom whenever she wants to make something. I like putting all the ingredients together and mixing it and watching it cook and then getting to eat something that tastes good at the end. But I pretend I don't like it."

"Why do you pretend you don't like it?"

"Because it's embarrassing. And my Dad would laugh at me."

"Cookies and cakes are awesome. Baking is cool and so are minerals and so are horses." Andy said.

"Yeah. Baking *is* cool."

"Plus, I'll bet it'll help you get girls when you're older."

"Yeah. And you'll be surrounded by girls too because they like horses."

I laughed. "Yeah!"

And that was the end of it. Andy and I mended what was broken. The rest of the summer flew by. I never went with Andy to horse riding lessons but I was often in the woods hunting minerals with him. And even though it should have been boring, it wasn't. Andy always made things fun.

He got better at skateboarding, too. I eventually asked him if there were any skate parks around here but he said no. So I ended up spending my time doing other stuff with Andy. Looking for rocks was even kind of fun.

For weeks I'd been pretending I wasn't nervous about my first day of 7th grade. Dad told me to buck up and deal, that thousands of kids were starting at a new school this year and if they could do it, I could do it. I knew he was right but I was still scared. Jake wasn't scared. He'd met a bunch of friends through Danny over the summer so he was going into our new school with a friend group. I hadn't met any of Andy's friends.

The night before my first day Andy and I played street hockey with Danny and Jake. We kicked their asses. Since the rules were loser had to clean up, Andy and I left them there with the equipment and climbed the hill back up to our houses.

66

Andy had been quieter the last couple days, which did nothing for my nerves.

Before I could ask him what was wrong, though, he asked me. "Are you nervous about tomorrow?"

I shrugged. "I guess. I'm more nervous I won't make friends." I realized how that sounded and rushed to explain. "Not that I need more friends! Just that, you know, you won't be in ALL of my classes so-"

"It's okay," he said. "You'll make friends, I promise."

"That's good." I sighed.

"I just hope you'll still be my friend."

"Of course, dude, we're best friends!"

"We are?" He asked, almost surprised.

"Yeah, you know that! Plus we found out last week that we have homeroom together. We're homies for life."

Andy started laughing. "For LIFE?"

"Yep." I stopped when I got to my garage. "See you at the bus stop tomorrow?"

Andy's face fell. "Oh no. My mom drives me to school."

"No, take the bus with me! I wont know any of those kids!"

"I can't. You can ride with me and my mom if you want."

"I wish. Dad says I have to take the bus to look after Jake."

"Oh, well..." Andy shrugged. "I'll just see you at school then?"

The bus wasn't bad the next morning. It was mostly just Danny pointing out the cool kids to make friends with and the weird kids to avoid. I found it strange that Danny took the bus while Andy didn't. But I didn't ask him about it.

I found my homeroom pretty quickly. Mr. Gage's class, room 333. I was there before Andy, so I sat at a desk that had lots of empty ones surrounding it. A kid with blonde hair and a Thrasher shirt sat down on the other side of me.

"New kid?" He asked casually. I could tell immediately he was probably one of the kings of the school.

"Yep. Moved this summer."

"From where?"

"Seattle."

"Seattle's the shit. Great skate scene there."

"Yep. I miss that. Wish there was somewhere to skate around here."

"There is. Me and my friends go there."

"To a skatepark? Around here?"

"Yeah, on Willow."

"That's like a mile from my house." Why the hell hadn't Andy told me? We could have been skating there all summer instead of looking for rocks and riding bikes into the pool.

"Cool. I'm Adam."

"I'm Eli."

"Cool."

The room continued to fill up, including the desks around me. Adam was like a beacon that other kids seemed to gravitate to. When I finally saw Andy walk through the door, there was only one desk left, the one in front of me. He looked nervous but I wasn't sure why until I heard it. The booing. A whole room of it.

Every kid, and I mean every *single* kid was booing Andy as he shuffled through the room to the seat in front of me. His face got red and he dropped his bag, looked back at me nervously, but otherwise ignored the booing. I did nothing. I said nothing. I didn't know how to react.

Mr. Gage walked in, then, and the booing ended immediately. After homeroom everyone shuffled out quickly and I only had time to say "see you at PE" to Andy.

Adam was in my next class and we talked more about skating. He introduced me to some of his other friends. One of them was a girl named Molly and I really liked her. She was pretty with black and purple hair.

PE was the last class before lunch. When I saw Andy he was looking down at the ground and standing alone. I walked directly over to him. "Are you okay?"

"Yeah," was all he said.

We stood together as the PE teacher explained we'd be playing kickball, a fun thing for the first day of school. She picked team captains. I was picked maybe 5th from the group. Andy was picked last. Everyone on his team groaned. His face turned red again. I hated those kids.

We didn't really get to talk through the rest of PE because we were on different teams. After PE we went back to the locker room together. I tried to talk to him as we changed clothes but he didn't want to say much.

"What do you think lunch today is?"

Andy shrugged.

"I hope it's pizza. Or hamburger."

"It's probably chicken." He mumbled.

"Ugh, I hate chicken. I wish-"

"Hey, Eli! What you doin' hanging out with the Horse Princess over there?" Adam had left Andy alone during PE but it seemed that just by talking to Andy I'd drawn attention to him.

I didn't know what to say so I settled for "What?"

"Dandy Andy, Princess of the land of horses and rubies. What are you doing hanging out with him?"

"Oh. Um, he's my neighbor."

I wasn't looking at Andy, but I could feel him stiffen. I tried to recover but the damage was done.

"I mean, we-"

"Sit at our table at lunch. We'll tell you about the skate park. It's dope. "

"Yeah okay."

Adam walked away and I turned to Andy. "Wanna sit with me at lunch?"

Andy didn't say anything.

"I'm sure they make fun of everybody, I'm sure they'll make fun of me, too. It's just for fun. Everyone rips on their friends."

"They're not my friends." Andy didn't look at me, just kept shoving gym clothes into his bag. "You sit with them if you want. I won't. They don't want me there."

"*I* want you there. Best friends, remember?"

"Do you?" Andy shot me a look and then walked away. He didn't sit with us at lunch. In fact, when I found him in the cafeteria, he was sitting at a table alone. It became very clear throughout the day that *everyone* at Copperfield hated Andy. But still I pretended I didn't notice it.

After I got off the bus I went to his house and rung the doorbell. He opened the door immediately, as if he'd been waiting for me.

"I'm sorry." I didn't even let him speak. "I know you're mad at me because I sat with Adam and those other guys at lunch. It's just that Adam is in most of my classes and...you're not but that doesn't mean anything."

"Okay," Andy shrugged.

I paused. "Why didn't you tell me about the skate park on Willow?"

Andy sighed. "Because Adam and his friends are always there. They hate me. They always make fun of me. I didn't want them to do that in front of you."

I frowned. "I'm sorry everyone at Copperfield is such a dick to you. But I'm not. I'm your friend. Forever, remember?"

"I thought you were getting rid of me as a friend 'cause I'm not cool like those guys. Please don't do that, I like having a friend! I haven't had a friend since 3rd grade. It's nice not to be alone. But today I felt alone again."

"Not tomorrow. Not any other day. I promise. Okay?"

"Yeah...okay."

"Should we go hunt for malware now?"

Andy smiled for the first time all day. "It's malachite."

We hunted for it, but we didn't find it. We never did. And I'm ashamed to say that the next day at school unfolded much like the first. I *did* sit with Andy at lunch but he was quiet and reserved. Adam and two of his friends mocked Andy from two tables away for being a "horse princess". I ignored them. And I didn't move away or leave Andy. But I didn't stick up for him either. I ended up finishing my food early. Andy left with me, dumping his lunch, uneaten, into the trash.

That afternoon I took the bus home and grabbed my skateboard from the garage. And then I met up with Adam, Brayden, and Molly at the skate park. I didn't tell Andy where I went, but it's not like we had plans.

The next day, Brayden took Andy's usual desk in home-room before he got there. I didn't tell Brayden to move. Andy sat on the other side of the classroom. I felt bad. But I also felt accepted. Adam's group was popular. I was becoming popular.

But really it was inevitable I would be friends with Adam and Brayden and the others. They were into skating and ska, like me. Andy wasn't, but we could still be friends. I was allowed to have multiple friends and I shouldn't feel bad about it.

As the weeks passed, Andy retreated more and more. We would go whole days without talking to each other. Sometimes after school I would go to Brayden's or Molly's. Andy was never invited. Sometimes, out of guilt, I would ring his doorbell. Mrs. Barden always told me Andy was out in the woods hunting gems. I never went to look for him. He probably wanted to be alone, anyway.

After awhile, I stopped trying to engage with Andy. I always saw him watching me. He looked sad, but not angry. I smiled at him when Adam wasn't looking. I tried to tell him we were still friends through my looks. I was just taking some space to make other friends as well. That was normal.

Dad seemed to like my new friends a lot. He was a strict dad, wanted his boys to be boys. And I knew whatever Jake said, Dad would never hit him. I knew that was a lie. Jake was just prone to stories, always trying to impress me. He was an old fashioned dad, but a good dad. He loved us. He loved Mom, too, I think. The only thing they ever fought about was her drinking.

Eventually, I learned from Dad that he never liked Andy. He called him "the pussy kid next door". He never said that in front of Jake and Danny. He said it to me, though. He was happy I wasn't hanging out with him anymore. I didn't agree with my dad. Andy was still my friend, even if we were taking some time apart.

And then came October 9th, a day I would remember for the ret of my life. We'd been in school for over a month. It wasn't a typical day, sunny for how late in the year it was. We had two subs that morning which meant a lot of dicking around. Andy didn't come to PE that day. He stayed in the locker room. We heard the coach say he felt sick. I knew that was a lie. It was kickball day again and I knew Andy was em-barrassed to be picked last.

It happened in the cafeteria over lunch. Adam and I were doing pretend skate tricks on the benches. Molly was watching me, giving me girl eyes. Both my brother and Danny were watching her. Everyone had a crush on Molly. But she was watching me.

When it happened, it was loud. The whole cafeteria shut up, turned toward the clatter, and then laughed. But only because it was Andy who dropped the tray. Anyone else would have been ignored or maybe ribbed a little. But everyone hated Andy.

"Having trouble with your hooves there, princess?" Adam yelled from two tables away. Andy ignored him and bent down to clean up his spilled tray.

"Yeah, shouldn't you be eating oats and hay?" Another kid yelled.

"Ewww." Came from a random girl. Andy's face turned beet red and he started breathing hard. I turned to Adam.

"Come on, man, leave him alone."

Adam's face went scarlet. Angry. "Sticking up for your girlfriend, Eli?"

"No. I'm just saying, who cares? So he likes horses. Cowboys like horses."

"Not sure you're making his case, dude. Ever see Brokeback Mountain?" Brayden asked.

"Yeah, maybe you're his cowboy boyfriend." Adam laughed. I looked over at Molly. She was laughing, too. At me. I looked at Andy. He was watching me. He knew what I was thinking. And he was begging me not to.

But Molly was still laughing, and this time it was at me.

So I did it. I said something unforgivable. Something I could never take back. Something I was never able to apologize for.

I raised my voice so more people would hear. "I saw his room once. He has posters of horses, he- he has statues of them, too. He decorates the statues with tiaras he made from all the rubies and emeralds he finds behind his house."

They all laughed. I didn't look at Andy. But I felt it, the devastation. I didn't look at him but I felt it all the same.

"And the thing is, he knows it's all make believe. All the 'gemstones' he finds are just rocks. He's just playing Horse Princess alone in his room." I finished.

"Ah, poor Dandy Andy. No friends." Adam yelled loud enough for the whole cafeteria to hear. This started a rousing chant of "Dandy Andy" from wall to wall. It was deafening.

I looked at Molly. She was laughing again, but this time it wasn't at me. Everyone was laughing and chanting, even Jake. Even Andy's little brother Danny was laughing. But not at me. No one was laughing at me now.

I heard a loud sob which drew my gaze back to Andy. He was crying, his face was even redder. He threw his tray on the ground and ran out of the cafeteria, the chorus of "Dandy Andy" following him down the hall. And I felt bad.

I decided I would apologize to him at home, like I always did. I would find him after school and do it. He would understand. Andy was good like that.

As soon as I cleared the bus door, I took off into the woods. I knew that's where he'd be. I found him in his usual spot, by the creek. Andy was digging like always, a pile of neatly stacked rocks next to him. He didn't look up as I approached. He didn't even acknowledge I was there.

"I'm sorry, okay?" Andy ignored me.

"Look, they were all laughing, I didn't know what to do. I was with my friends and everyone already doesn't like you, you know? So what I said didn't really do any damage. They already thought that stuff, anyway. It was just logical, you know?"

He opened his mouth to say something but the deafening horn of a nearby train drowned out whatever it was. I felt the rumble under my feet.

"What?!" I yelled when his mouth stopped moving.

"You're a bad friend, Eli!"

"No I'm not!"

"Yes you are, a totally shitty friend!"

I grew angry, then. "I'm your *only* friend, Andy!"

"I'd rather have no friends than a friend like you!"

"Oh really? Are you sure you want to do this? I'm all you've got!"

"You're not a friend to me, anyway! I thought you were but you ignore me. You laugh at me and make fun of me just like they do!"

"Well...shit, Andy, maybe if you tried harder! Stop with the horses and digging in the dirt for gems!"

"No! I like those things! They don't laugh at me or lie to me!" I stared at him, trying to come up with something to say. "Just leave me alone, Eli."

"Well, well...fine! Be a pussy with your princess horses and fucking gemstones. This is the most sissy shit I've ever seen! Mining for pretty rocks! It's pathetic! You'll never be cool or popular! 'Cause of your pussy-ass hobbies!"

I kicked it. I kicked his whole pile of mined stones into the water behind him. I knew he'd been collecting them for months. Andy screamed and dove after them. He wailed as he tried to catch the rocks before the current buried them or took them away.

And I left him there. Andy's sobs followed me out of the woods along with his screams.

"I hate you! I hate you, Elliot! You're the pussy and I hate you!"

When I walked into my backyard, Dad was standing on the patio smoking. He nodded at me, and then he smiled. He'd probably heard it all, the whole fight with Andy. And it was clear he approved of what I'd done. I felt sick. I went to my room. I listened to music and I fell asleep early. Angry and confused.

I never saw Andy alive again. I'd learn later that he never left those woods.

Andy wasn't at school the next day. And I'm ashamed to say I was relieved. I didn't want to face him after the things I'd said. It was a good day, otherwise, without Andy there to stare at me and make me feel bad.

It was just after lunch that the murmuring began. Hushed whispers behind tightly cupped hands. The teachers had a secret. Everyone noticed and there was much speculation about what it was.

At 5th period we found out classes were canceled for the rest of the day and we were having an assembly. I felt nauseous when I walked into the auditorium. Andy wasn't at school and there was an emergency assembly.

He's run away, I thought. *He's run away and I know where he went. I can help.* I decided that as soon as the assembly ended I would find my teacher and tell them Andy went to Wyoming. That he wanted to start a ranch there. The Rocking A Ranch.

I sat next to Adam, Molly on my other side. She touched me, for the first time, I think. It barely registered, though. I waited to hear about Andy.

A police officer and our principal walked onto stage together. They wasted no time at all.

"We've gathered everyone here because we have some very sad news and we wanted to get in front of the rumors. Last night, one of your fellow students passed."

"Passed?" I whispered to no one in particular. "What does that mean, 'passed'?"

"It means they're dead, dumbass." I heard someone reply. I let go of a long breath. So this wasn't about Andy after all.

"How'd they die?" Someone up front yelled.

The principal took a deep breath and let it out. He looked conflicted, like he didn't know what to say. The cop stepped in.

"Suicide. It's a very sad and serious matter. Andy Barden took his own life last night. It's very sad and we'd like to speak to anyone who was close to him."

There was a buzzing in my ears. It was loud. But I could still hear the snickering and whispering and giggling.

"....horse heaven".

"...giant pussy..."

"I knew he'd do it."

A few people toward the back started a low chant of "Dandy Andy". The buzzing in my head got louder. I felt nothing.

Mom picked me up from school that day. I think I was still in shock. I hadn't said much to anyone. But I asked her if it was true, if Andy had killed himself last night. Mom was a little drunk. She said "Yes, that poor boy. Laid right down there to die."

"Laid down where? Where did he die, Mom?"

But she just mumbled over and over about what a shame it was and how she needed to send a fruit basket to the Barden's.

Dad was on the back patio when I got home. I begged him to tell me what happened. He did so mater-of-factly, while looking out into the woods behind the house.

"Laid himself down on the tracks. Rocks in his hands, arms at his sides. Train came, trains always come. Guys in the engineering car said they blew the horn." He shook his head. "Kid didn't move. Didn't flinch. He wanted that train to hit him. And it did. Tore him apart."

6000 tons of angry machine had run over Andy. Killed him. Because of what I'd said to him. Because I kicked his rocks into the creek. Because he thought his only friend hated him. But I'd never hated him. And I didn't get to tell him that.

I threw up in front of my dad. He shook his head, probably in disgust, and went inside.

My mom wailed about "that poor boy next door" for weeks. Dad didn't bring it up again. Cops talked to me since I was the only person close to Andy. I told them the truth, mostly. Not about kicking his rocks into the creek. They closed his case. Jake spent a lot of time with Danny, who had lost a brother. And then the Barden's moved across town, away from the tracks that killed their son.

As for me, the years just passed. Guilt and liquor and sex and drugs. All the things Andy would never get to experience. I dated Molly, she cheated on me. I got into a fist fight with Adam. I fucked him up and his family sued me. Brayden went to juvie for stealing. Jake became popular. So did Danny. They were on the same track as me, cool kids who ruled their grade. I graduated. I got a job at Jack in the Box.

I thought about Andy a lot. About how sad he must have been, how dead inside to lay down on cold, metal train tracks and wait for a train to run him over. I thought about how much I must have hurt him. With time, grew understanding. It was my fault. I'd been a piece of shit, a bully. I was the one who deserved the tracks, not Andy, who just wanted to ride horses and dig for gemstones. Andy, who never hurt anybody and never told them I liked baking, even if it would made them laugh at me instead.

And quicker than you would have thought, everyone forgot about him. No one ever said Andy's name in all those years. And no one probably ever would have again if it wasn't for a conversation I overheard in the parking lot of the Jack in the Box one day.

It was just one guy talking to a cop. The cop was sitting in his car and the other man was leaning over talking to him through the window. I was crouched down against the wall, smoking a cigarette. Based on the conversation, they couldn't sec me there.

"This is something you said you could do." The man said, his voice hushed, but angry.

"I didn't tell you that. Take up your marker with Onwitt."

"He said to talk to you."

The cop leaned closer to the man. "Your kid killed someone."

"That lady was homeless!"

"Doesn't matter. He was drunk, she was on the side-walk, and he creamed her. That can't be buried. Everyone knows the facts of the case. A video is on facebook, for fucks sake."

"You can make this go away. What if toxicology comes back negative for alcohol? What if he swerved to avoid hitting a dog?"

"That's a lot of favors."

"I'll pay."

"You can't afford it, even with your marker."

"Bull. Shit. I know you did it before. For someone else. That case from years ago, the kid on the tracks."

The cop cracked his door open, shoving the man back with it. He got right in his face. "Lower your fucking voice. That was a suicide."

"Yeah, I'd like to know how that kid walked through the woods and laid down on some tracks with half his head caved in."

I didn't breathe. I didn't move. I couldn't think. So I waited. The cop let the man go and shoved him into the side of the car.

"Talk to Onwitt. Although I don't know why he'd want to help you seeing as you've got a big fucking mouth."

The cop drove off then. The other man got into his truck and drove away as well, not knowing the nuclear bomb they'd left behind.

They had to have been talking about Andy. He was the only kid on the tracks that I knew about. And according to that guy Andy'd already been dead when the train hit him. Which means somebody killed Andy. That's why he didn't move when the train blew it's horn. He was already gone.

Somebody had killed him... Holy shit.

Not only that, somebody had covered it up. I threw my cigarette on the ground and went back into work. I told my boss I was feeling sick. I knew he didn't believe me but he let me go. He couldn't fire me. Nobody else wanted this shit job.

I went home and paced around my room. Somebody had murdered Andy that night. Who had known he was out in the woods? I sat down at my desk and pulled out a notebook from my senior year. I found a clean page and started writing. Who'd known...

Mrs. Barden.

My Dad.

I tapped my pencil. There was one other person who knew. It was pointless but I added another name:

Me.

I didn't hurt Andy so that left Andy's mom and my dad. Andy's mom wouldn't do it. She loved Andy. My dad wouldn't murder a kid. He hated Andy but he would never kill him. He was happy we weren't friends anymore. He was satisfied. But more than that, Dad left shortly after I came inside and went to the bar with his friends.

That meant that someone must have stumbled onto Andy out in the woods. He was screaming and crying loudly. Someone must have heard him and that...that could have been anyone.

So I added to the list:

Everyone else.

Fuck. What else did I know?

I knew that the police *knew* it was a murder and they listed it as a suicide. They covered up the murder for someone.

It could be anyone. Everyone hated Andy. I squeezed my pencil tighter.

Focus.

So, who would the police want to help? Someone with money. Someone with a marker, whatever that was.

But then, I remembered Mr. Barden was a cop, and the whole thing made no sense again. Andy told me his dad had been a cop for more than twenty years. That meant he probably had a lot of seniority. Why would he let them cover up his son's murder? It didn't make any fucking sense.

I ripped the paper out of the notebook and threw it in the trash. Dad had friends who were cops. Maybe he would know.

I found my dad out on the patio drinking a Coors. He was on the phone with someone. The tone of his voice made me think it was a woman. Mom was home, but drunk. My parents had almost divorced years before when Mom caught my Dad cheating. Didn't seem like much had changed. Dad sat up straighter when he saw me.

"Gotta go. I'll give you a call later."

.....

"Yeah, I'm gonna be up there but it's boys night. So maybe another night."

.....

"We'll talk about it later, quit your yellin'."

Dad hung up and set his phone on the armrest of his chair. Then he leaned back and stared at me.

"Somethin' on your mind, Eli?"

He was curious, maybe a little suspicious. I never really talked to him anymore. But this was important.

"Yeah, I have a question."

His brows turned down. "Don't get involved in my business, son."

"This isn't about you."

"Alright," Dad leaned back in his chair and lit a cigarette. He blew the smoke out loudly. "So what's it about?"

"It's about Andy."

"The kid who kilt himself when y'all were 12?"

"He didn't kill himself."

Dad frowned. "What are you talking about?"

I took a deep breath. "He was dead before the train hit him. Andy was murdered and someone covered it up. Pretended it was a suicide and everyone went along with it."

Dad raised an eyebrow. Then he mumbled, "Your mom should've gotten you a therapist."

"It's true, Dad. Andy was murdered."

"And where'd you hear that?"

"In town."

"Alright. So you got caught up in some gossip about an 8 year old suicide and now you believe it was a murder."

"It *was* a murder. Andy was murdered before he was put on the tracks! Someone found him alone in the woods and killed him!" I stood up quickly and started pacing around the porch.

"Alright, son, calm down. Tell me how you think I can help here."

"The cops covered it up. Why would they do that? Who would they cover it up for?"

"No one. I'm friends with a lot of the boys, they're good people. They say that boy killed himself, he did."

"What's a marker, Dad?"

He sighed. "It's a favor."

"What kinds of people have markers with the police?"

Dad narrowed his eyes at me. "The kind that could get you in trouble. Drop it, Eli."

"But-"

"Just drop it! Do not ask questions like that." Dad was angry, red-faced. His voice shook.

"Dad, I just-"

"No. No more talking about this. That boy committed suicide. He was weak in mind and body. Always crying. It's sad but it's over."

"It is *not* over." I said through my teeth. Dad was up out of his chair and in my face in an instant.

"You wanna push this? Open your mouth? Spread around town that boy was murdered? Because near as I remember it, you were the last person seen with him. Fightin' with him. How's that gonna look, Eli?"

"I didn't do anything."

Dad stared me down. "Didn't you?"

My face got hot. I stumbled back, just a step, but it was enough.

"It is not in your best interest to pursue this, Elliot."

"I didn't do anything," I repeated, though it was weaker, quieter.

"Yeah. Keep on telling yourself that like you always have. Drop this."

I didn't say anything. I turned around and walked off the patio. Walked right into the woods and kept on walking.

I went to the creek. I remembered where it was, even though I hadn't been there in 8 years. Elliot's spot. There was no stack of rocks and no holes in the bank of the creek. Everything

Andy had left behind was gone. No one talked about Andy. And now it seemed even nature had forgotten him.

I remembered everything about that day. We argued. I kicked his rocks into the water. I *walked away*. I know I did. I remembered doing it. Those were real memories. I wouldn't have hurt Andy.

Except...I did. With what I said to him.

There was a deep tremor underneath my feet. I felt the train before I heard it. I didn't know where on the tracks Andy was been when he was hit. I couldn't visit the spot he'd died. So I turned around and walked back out of the woods.

I couldn't sleep that night. I had nightmares of Andy being murdered. Half his head missing. I needed to know how he'd died. I'd failed Andy on so many levels when we were kids. I wasn't going to fail him in this.

The next day at work was slow. I had a lot of time to think about all the people who hated Andy. Not because Andy ever did anything wrong. But because someone found out a boy liked horses in 3rd grade and laughed at him. And then other kids joined in. And then it was cool to hate Andy. But who would have taken it further?

After work I went to the police station. I thought maybe I could ask for the files of the case. The coroners report. I should have known better. The man at the desk shut me down. No. Those weren't available for the public. Only the family could request them.

I wasn't as close to Danny as I had been when we were in school, hanging out in the same group. He never came around the house anymore since he and Jake had had a falling out a year before. But I knew he was Jake's age - only 17. Danny couldn't request the files.

Danny's dad was a cop. He would have access. But there was a chance he knew about the coverup. But then, there was no reason for him to cover up his son's murder. Perhaps he didn't even know. There was a chance he would be as upset as I was.

But it wasn't Danny's dad who answered the door. It was Mrs. Barden and she was surprised to see me.

"Um, is Mr. Barden home?"

"Eli. My goodness. No, I'm afraid he's at work. Would you like to come in?"

"Oh um. Well..."

She let go of the door and sagged against the wall. "Wow. I haven't seen you since we moved." She smiled sadly. "I wonder what Andy would have looked like at your age. He was such a handsome boy."

It was an in, and I took it. "Actually, I had some questions about Andy. That's why I came over, I wanted to ask Mr. Barden some stuff."

She looked confused but opened the door all the way, inviting me inside. "Well, you knew Andy was well as anyone. I'm not sure what questions you have about him but I am happy to answer them. No one ever mentions Andy anymore." She said tearfully.

Oh god, she was crying. I had to do this. I had to do this.

We sat down at her kitchen table and she offered me coffee.

"So, what would you like to know, Eli?"

I took a deep breath, in and out. "I heard..." I swallowed. "I heard there's the possibility that maybe the official ruling of 'suicide' was wrong."

Mrs. Barden said nothing. The grip around her coffee mug became tight, making her fingers white.

"You...you heard someone is challenging the suicide ruling?"

"No. I just heard that..."

"What? What did you hear, Eli?" She set her mug down and her white hands wrapped around mine. Her fingers were so cold, even though she'd just been holding a hot mug.

"Just that maybe Eli was already dead when he was laid on the tracks."

She was silent and still. "Where did you hear this?"

"Some people in town."

Her grip tightened. "Who in town?" My hands started to hurt. I tried to pull them away, but she squeezed harder.

"Who, Eli?"

"I don't know who they were. Have you heard that before? That Andy was murdered?"

She jerked her hands back. "I don't know what you're talking about. I've never heard that before."

I said nothing, just watched her. She was scared. She knew something. *Fuck.* I got angry. I yanked my hands back, knocking my coffee mug onto the floor, spilling it everywhere.

"You *knew*. You knew Andy was murdered. *You fucking knew!*"

"Eli, you cannot talk like this. For your own sake, and mine."

"Why are you letting this happen? Why are you letting your son's murderer walk free?"

"You don't understand."

"You're a mother! His fucking mother!"

"Eli, this situation is more complicated than you think."

"What's complicated? The fact that you're the shittiest fucking mother I've ever seen?"

She slapped me then, right across the face. I didn't feel it. "You know NOTHING about what kind of mother I am!"

"Your husband go along with this? Let his own son's murder be covered up? And you support that?"

"We're doing this *for* Andy!"

"You don't make any fucking sense. Who did it?"

"Stop."

"Who did it, Mrs. Barden? Who killed your son? Who caved his head in and then laid him on a pair of cold, metal tracks to be ripped apart by a fucking train?"

"Stop! Please, just stop!" Her hands were cupped over her ears. She was breaking.

"Tell me!"

"You of all people should not be asking these questions, Elliot!"

"Tell me who killed Andy!"

"Please! Please stop asking me! Don't make me, please-"

"Who murdered your son?!"

A large hand clamped down on my shoulder. "Time to go." I heard my father say into my ear. He hauled me back and out the door as tears spilled down my face. I'd been close.

I heard my dad on the phone with somebody, probably Mr. Barden, telling him to come home and manage his wife. Dad dragged me into the house and slammed the door to my bedroom, him inside.

He said nothing.

"You know, too, don't you. You know who killed Andy" I said.

"Yes."

I sobbed. "Who? Who killed him?"
Silence.

"Why did the cops agree to cover it up? Was it money?"

"No."

"A marker?"

"Eli."

"Did the police owe someone a favor?!"

"No. Goddamit, Eli, just shut up!"

"Why? Why should I be silent?!"

"Have you considered that the person being protected is *you?*"

"What did I do?" I sobbed.

"Christ, what indeed."

I didn't say anything, just silently cried.

"You know, of both of my sons, you were always the softest."

I took a moment to try and compose myself. "Jake said you used to hit him."

Dad nodded. "That's right. I saw the mistakes I made with you and I wanted him to turn out better."

"You beat my little brother?" My voice cracked.

"I never beat him, Eli. I disciplined him. After I had no hope for you."

I shook my head, wiping my face with my sleeve. "Are you that disappointed in me?"

He leaned back against the door. "Not anymore. Not since the day you came out of the woods, angry, fuming, that kid from next door crying and hollarin' for everyone to hear. I thought you'd turned a corner. Thought you'd keep better company. Be a man."

I scoffed. "If you are what a 'man' is in this town, I don't wanna be one anyway."

I shoved past him and yanked the door open. He caught my sleeve. "You drop this whole thing with the Barden kid, you hear?"

"Why?" I spat.

He leaned in close. I could smell the stale smoke on his breath. "Because you couldn't handle the truth of what happened to him. And you huntin' for that truth is gonna hurt a lot of people you don't wanna hurt."

I pushed the door open and left him there, in my room. "Oh, and Eli?" Dad said from behind me. I stopped and turned my head, just a little, to show I was listening. "I want you out of this house by Friday. For good."

I turned the corner and started down the stairs, running smack into Jake. "What did he just say? Is he- is Dad kicking you out?"

"Yeah." I said.

"What- what the fuck, why? Where you gonna go?" Jake's voice shook a little. He was 17 but still relied on me a lot. He was scared of Dad, scared of graduating, scared of ending up an outcast like so many others. Small towns were fickle and we both knew it.

I hadn't even begun to process what being kicked out meant. But right at that moment, I knew it meant not being there for Jake.

"I don't know."

"We could get a place together?" He said desperately.

"Dad would never allow that. You're 17 for another 8 months."

"I'll piss him off, too. What did you do? I could get kicked out!"

I hugged him. I never hugged my brother; Dad thought it was 'gay'. But today, I did. And he hugged me back. "You'll be okay, Jake." I heard him give a little heave. I knew he was scared.

"You can't leave me here."

"It's okay," I whispered into his ear. "You can cry with me."

He heaved again. "Don't tell dad." He said quietly.

"I won't." I promised.

I left while Jake was at school on Thursday. I couldn't say goodbye, it was too painful. I left him a note telling him I loved him and that I'd send him my address as soon as I found a new place. I moved two towns over. I sent Jake my address. He never responded. Maybe he was mad at me for sneaking away while he was at school. Maybe he was mad I hadn't taken him with me. Or maybe Dad had gotten to him.

I worked, had a shitty apartment. Things got better. I dated a girl I met out one night. She didn't cheat on me. I married her a year later. We had a kid, little girl. Then we divorced. She wanted to move to Denver. I saw my kid in the summers.

Met another girl. Dated her for years. She left me because I didn't wanna get married again.

Jake ended up in jail for a year. He wrote me letters. He'd finally fought back against Dad. Hurt Dad real bad. But I knew that fucker deserved it. Jake got out of jail. He moved in with me. Dad sent him letters. The fucked up thing, Dad said he was proud of Jake for finally standing up to him. Dad never said a word about me. Jake met a girl online and moved to Chicago to be with her. They got married, had a couple kids. Jake's in real estate now, makes good money. He's nothing like Dad. I visit them a couple times a year.

It's been 13 years since I left Ralling, 21 since Andy died. I never went back. I never tried to request any records. I never talked about Andy. So, I'd failed him once again. I'd never know who killed Andy, or why. I'd never know why it was covered up. No one was talking. And no one ever would.

I still think about Andy a lot. I lay awake at night, drunk, and sometimes crying, begging forgiveness for failing him in so many ways. Andy had a sad life. There was very little good and a short, painful end. There would never be a Rocking A Ranch. Andy would always just be a murder victim with a closed case.

No one had to pay for it. And no one ever would.

So, I guess the moral of this story is that sometimes the world isn't fair. There's injustice and corruption and the universe doesn't always bother to balance it out. Andy's murder was just more sand poured on the cosmic scale in favor of evil. The scale sinks lower, the world gets shittier. And Andy rots in the ground, skull smashed in, body torn apart. And the world keeps spinning.

AFTERNOON OF OCTOBER 9TH

Eli: "...this is the most sissy shit I've ever seen! Mining for pretty rocks! It's pathetic! You'll never be cool or popular! 'Cause of your pussy-ass hobbies!"

Andy: "I hate you! I hate you, Elliot! You're the pussy and I hate you!"

Somebody snickers quietly. Another person shushes them, shuffling as they listen from nearby. They approach as Andy continues to cry, fishing his rocks out of the creek. Suddenly, they speak.

Danny: "Lost your only friend, Dandy Andy?"

Andy: "Shut up, Danny. Go away."

Jake: "Sounds like even Eli thinks you're a loser now."

Andy: "Eli is a loser!"

Jake pushes Andy back into the creek.

Jake: "Don't talk about my brother like that. He says you're a pussy, that means you're a pussy!"

Andy: "Stop it! He didn't mean it! He doesn't think I'm a pussy!"

Andy crawls out of the creek.

Andy: "He's just mad. We're friends. We fight sometimes."

Danny shoves Andy back in the water.

Andy: "Stop pushing me into the creek!"

Danny: "No."

Jake: "You belong in the creek you fucking pussy."

They push him again.

Andy: "Stop it, you guys!"

Jake: "Fucking make us!"

Andy: "Fine, I will! See how you like it!"

A rock flies through the air and cracks against a tree.

Danny: "Oh hell no, did you just throw a rock at us?"

Jake: "I'm more impressed the princess was willing to part with one of her gems."

Andy, crying: "Shut up! Just shut up!"

Another stone goes flying. THUD.

Jake: "Oh hell no, he just fucking hit me! You got mud on my fucking vans!"

Danny: "You're fucked now, pussy."

Andy: "No, I didn't mean it! You guys were throwing rocks at me, you started it!"

Jake and Danny rush into the creek and push Andy down.

Andy: "Stop it! I'm sorry, okay? I'm sorry!"

Jake: "Gimme a rock, a big one."

Danny picks up a giant rock.

Danny: "This one's pretty big."

Andy: "Please, don't!"

Jake: " How do you like that, huh? A muddy rock smeared all over your face? Don't you love it?"

Andy: "Stop it!"

Danny: "Don't you love these rocks? They're so precious to you, Dandy Andy."

Andy spits in Jake's face.

Jake: "Did you just spit in my fucking face, pussy?!"

Andy: "There was mud in my mouth!"

Danny: "You just spit in his fucking face!"

Danny throws a heavy rock into Andy's rib cage.

Danny: "I wish you'd just die! It's embarrassing to be your brother, just fucking run away from home!"

Jake: "Get his pretty boy face!"

Danny hits Andy's face with the rock.

Jake: "Here, let me try."

Danny: "It's hilarious, look at the faces he's making."

More hits.

Andy: "Eli will hurt you when he finds out what... what you're doing."

Jake: "Shut up! Eli doesn't give a fuck about you! You're a loser! He loves me and he hates you!"

They continue to pound Andy with rocks.

Jake: "I heard him say it! He hates you, he hates you!"

Danny: "Dude."

Jake: "My brother hates you!"

Danny: "Stop! Stop!"

Danny tackles Jake off of Andy.

Danny: "Look at his fucking face!"

Jake: "Is he…"

Danny: "Is he what?"

Jake: "Is he dead?"

Danny, scared: "I don't know. Look at his fuckin' head."

Jake: "He is...he's dead."

Danny: "You killed him!"

Jake: "You helped!"

Danny: "What do we do? Oh shit, what do we do?"

Jake: "Maybe my brother-"

Danny: "No, fuck that. Maybe we can...hide it or something. Or hide what we did."

Jake: "How? It's a dead body!"

They hear a train horn in the distance.

EVENING OF OCTOBER 9TH

Jake: "I didn't do anything!"

Jake's Dad: "Lower your voice or you'll wake your brother."

Danny: "We didn't do anything!"

Jake's Dad: "I saw you boys come back from the woods, wet and covered in mud. Then I get a call from *your* dad, Danny, looking for both his sons. Well, here you are, and now I'm hearin' about a body out on the tracks. You know who's not here? Andy. So you two are gonna tell me what the fuck happened."

Silence. Jake starts crying.

Jake: "We didn't mean to! He just kept yelling and we just kept hitting him! He just, he- he's weird and even Eli hates him now, too! He was a loser. Eli thinks so, we heard him!"

Danny: "You can't tell my dad!"

Jake: "Eli didn't even like him anymore, nobody's gonna miss him!"

Jake's Dad: "Both of you shut the fuck up. You think the cops ain't gonna be able to tell that body was dead before it got hit by a train?"

Jake: "No.. Dad, please. I don't wanna go to jail. It was...we heard Eli saying all that stuff. Really it's Eli's fault!"

Danny: "It wasn't our fault!"

Jake's Dad: "Shut your mouths. Danny, I'm calling your dad over here and we're gonna explain this 'accident'. He'll go along with fixin' this. He ain't gonna wanna lose two sons tonight."

Jake: "And...and Eli?"

Jake's Dad: "No. We ain't ever gonna tell Eli."

FALL

My usual smoke spot was off the Northeastern trail, next to a little creek where I could watch the fish as I got high. The trail itself was boring and flat, and the views were unimpressive even though it was dubbed the "Lake Loop". People rarely took the Northeastern trail so I was used to having it all to myself.

But that day I decided to take the *Western* trail. I shouldn't have done that.

My name's Kevin. I work at PepBoys, still live at home, and I get stoned after work everyday. Pretty sure my mom knows I do, but I like to hit the Chicago parks to smoke, anyway. You know, out in nature.

The day I took the Western trail had been a rough one. I'd forgotten to tighten a radiator cap and a lady came back with a smoking engine. My boss yelled at me in front of everyone, including the customer, which was fucking embarrassing. Because I can't quit this job. I need this job.

I decided to spend some extra time with my bowl that day. I parked in my usual spot next to the bathrooms and walked toward the Northeastern trailhead. Used to the solitude, I legitimately jumped when I heard a screech and then a shout behind me. I turned just in time to avoid a toddler who was being chased by an overwrought man in his 30's.

"Slow down, Jayden! Wait for your mother and your sisters!"

A shrill cry pulled my attention to a belabored woman slamming the trunk of a Mazda nearby. Two crying girls were pulling at her arms.

"No, don't make me, there's spiders!"

"There's spiders in the backyard too, Ava."

"But Mommy!"

"Monkeys! Monkeys!" The little boy shouted as he was scooped up in his father's arms.

"No monkeys here, buddy."

"Monkeys!" The kid screamed so loud I think I went deaf for a moment.

So, the Western trail it was.

I hadn't walked it often, preferring the even, easy path of the Lake Loop. The Western wound up into the hills which meant more cardio and less relaxation. Still, it was better than the other option... I pivoted, smiled, and sent the woman a little two fingered salute before making my way over to the entrance of the Western trail.

I walked for about twenty minutes - all uphill - before I split off from the trail on what looked like a well-used deer path. It was another ten before I found a good spot. It was just a little clearing with a fallen tree and a good view of the park. I pulled out my bowl, packed it, and flipped open my zippo. Inhaling the Northern Lights, I let it all melt away. My boss, my shitty car, my basement "apartment", and even those kids from the parking lot. It all floated away from me like the smoke on the breeze.

It was a gorgeous day for this early in the spring and I stayed for maybe half an hour to take it all in. Eventually, though, I packed it up. The sun was getting close to the horizon and it was a couple miles back to my car, all downhill or not. I stood up and stretched, liking this smoke spot but perhaps not as much as my usual where I could watch the fish.

It was pretty, though, so I decided to take a few pictures before I left. The trees, the sky, the fallen log. They made good pictures. And if I had left after taking them, none of it ever would have happened. I would have driven home and gone to bed. I would still have my crappy job. I would still drive my shitty car. I would still watch the fish when I got high.

Unfortunately, though, my eyes caught the way the sinking sunlight was filtering gold through some trees down the hillside. It looked incredible. And I had to take a picture of that, too.

So I walked over toward the edge. The ground was covered in undergrowth and moss...there was no way to see it. Until I felt it. On the fifth step my foot went down, as normal, but then it kept going. Sinking. And when I stumbled, my other foot caught up to the stuck one, and it sunk into the ground, too.

I fell forward and caught myself on my hands, phone flying into the underbrush. The jarring on my body sent my legs even deeper into the ground. Up to my knees.

I wasn't sinking, not exactly. No...it was a hole. A deep hole. And I was stuck halfway in it.

I twisted to pull my legs out but that only made me sink deeper. So deep, I was up to my waist. The hole was tight, pinching around my hips in a punishing grip.

I kicked my legs against the sides of the hole, trying to get enough purchase to leverage myself out. My feet scraped the dirt walls but found nothing to push against. I couldn't lift my knees. I braced my hands against the ground and pushed as hard as I could trying to lift myself out. I gained an inch but when I relaxed my arms to try again, I sunk deeper into the hole.

Much deeper.

The ground gripped my body so tightly that I finally started to panic. I was now sunken into the hole up to my armpits. Only my shoulders, arms, and head remained above ground. The dirt was like a vice around me. My chest was so constricted, I couldn't even get a full breath into my lungs.

I reached for the grass and pulled. The stalks broke in my hands. I took bigger handfuls of it. I felt the dirt around my chest shift. Jesus Christ, it was working. I let go intending to put my hands flat on the ground and push. Before I could even blink my body fell further down the hole. All the way down...

I was now in the dark. I couldn't see. My arms were above my head, shoulders folded in at an unnatural angle.

I was completely enveloped in the hole. No one would be able to see me from the surface.

It was hardly big enough for my body. I couldn't lift my knee, not even half an inch. My head was stuck between my chest and shoulders in such a way that I couldn't even look up toward the sky. And I still couldn't breathe all the way in.

So I panicked.

"Help!" I yelled down into my chest, voice cracking. I tried to take another breath, one deep enough to really scream. But I could only take half breaths. I slipped down a little more and the hole felt even smaller. But still I was slipping, being crushed in from the sides as the hole tapered more and more. I yelled again, as loud as I could. "Help me! Please! Help!"

I kicked my feet against the walls. They scraped against them. More dirt. I fell a little more. I started to have trouble breathing. I was encased in a tube of rock almost twenty feet under- ground at this point.

What if this hole went on forever? What if I died in here. I started to hyperventilate. There was no room to move at all now. I nodded my head back and forth between the wall and my shoulders which were behind my head. If I pushed, really pushed, possibly tore a muscle, I could look up and scream in the direction of the surface.

I could feel the muscles stretching and aching behind my shoulder blades as tipped my head back. I could feel them pulling, tearing, but still I continued. I felt the wall hit the back of my head and I blinked away the pain in my shoulders. Looking up...I saw light. But it was far away. I had fallen much further down the hole then I'd thought.

There wasn't even room for me to sob. There wasn't enough air to breathe. My ribs were pinched. My vision was clouding. I wasn't getting enough oxygen and my lungs started to burn.

I licked my lips and inhaled again, the millimeter or so that I could. My scream came out as a squeak but at least in the right direction: up. "Somebody help me please!"

The please was barely out of my mouth before I was falling again. I went down another ten feet or so before the walls suddenly open up. I crashed hard into solid ground and cried out as I hit the side of my hip. I lay for a couple of minutes in the dark, catching my breath now that I could actually breath again. I rolled onto my back and looked up.

The surface was only a pinpoint of light now. It was very, very far away.

"Fuck. Oh fuck, oh fuck, oh fuck." I started to shake. I had no idea what the fuck I was going to do. Where I was. Or how to get out. I reached over and massaged my hip, which pulled on my shoulder and the torn muscles there. If I had to guess, I would say my hip was bruised but not broken. What *was* broken, however was my bowl. I pulled the broken pieces out of my pocket and threw them into the darkness. They hit a wall nearby.

I pulled out my zippo. It took me two tries to light it be-cause my hands were shaking. But when I finally did, I was able to get a lock at the chamber I had fallen into.

It was small, maybe 6 feet by 8 feet; the walls, floor, and ceiling made of dirt. It wasn't a naturally occurring formation in the ground. I knew that because there were strange scratch marks in the corners and no rock in the chamber, only carved-out dirt. Something had made this.

And then there was the nest in the corner.

It was also made of dirt, loosely packed and high on the sides. There were patches of fur from various animals littered around the nest and next to it, another hole. This one was slightly big- ger than the hole I had just fallen through and it led down at an angle, not a vertical drop like the one in the ceil-ing.

I looked back up at the hole I'd fallen through. The light from outside was now purple - dusk. "Help!" I screamed. "Help me!"

I sat there yelling up at the hole until the light went from purple to gray to nonexistent. I yelled over and over. I yelled until I was hoarse. "Somebody fucking help me!"

Eventually I was silent, hours later, just lying on my back looking up at the ceiling. I used the zippo on and off. I tried to conserve the fuel, only using it when the darkness pressed in too much. In the deep of night I drifted off for a moment and when I awoke the light from the hole seemed to be turning gray again. That meant day. Day meant people. I watched as the gray warmed to a pink color.

I decided to try and collect pieces of my bowl and smoke out of it just to keep the worst of the panic at bay. I was on my hands and knees feeling around for the bowl when I heard it. The scratching. Something was moving. Something was coming through the hole in the wall next to the nest. It scratched as it scurried - and then it trilled.

I didn't move. Chances are whatever the animal was, it could see me in the dark, but who knew? I remained stretched, reaching out toward the glass, my shoulders burning. The thing scratched along the wall toward its nest. I remained still. And then I heard a piece of glass go spinning.

The thing made a shrill shriek, not unlike the kids from the parking lot. It was angry, I think. The thing kept shrieking, the sound ear-piercing. Suddenly I heard it run across the room, scamper up the wall, and then it was walking across the ceiling somehow.

It trilled again. The sound right over my head. But still I didn't move. I just raised my eyes to the ceiling, bracing for it. The light from the hole was brighter. Day was here. I could see the animal, but just barely.

It was larger than I expected. The hole it had come through was very small so it must be able to warp its body to fit through tight spaces. The shadow on the ceiling above me was maybe the size of a large boar, but had long arms and legs like a primate. It didn't look like it had hair, or a tail, but the features were impossible to make out.

I *could* tell that it was looking at me. Before my eyes could adjust further, the animal suddenly shrieked in my face. I fell back, scuttling toward the wall. The light from the ceiling disappeared and I realized that the creature was in the hole.

I pressed my hands against my mouth and bit down on my palm. *Don't fucking scream.* I had never seen an animal like that. Ever.

After a few minutes I noticed the light had returned. Either the thing was on the surface...or it had come back down into the room with me.

My eyes adjusted to the light again and I looked around. Nothing.

I crawled to the center of the room and looked up, screaming. For help, for rescue. For some- one to know I was down there. I screamed until I lost my voice. But no one screamed back.

Eventually I picked up all the pieces of my bowl. I tried to smoke it and when that didn't work, I ate the weed. I was thirsty, hungry, and terrified. And I was alone.

By now I had been a no show at work and my friends were probably calling me. My phone was on still on the surface, but I hoped someone would be able to track it. The cops or the FBI or something. My mom wouldn't worry start to worry for another few days.

As the light in the hole again cooled to gray, I started to accept what few options I had. I could stay in this cavern and scream upwards for help until I died of dehydration. Or I could go through the hole. Not the one I had come down. There was no way to reach it. The other hole. The one next to the nest that led even deeper underground ground. Maybe there would be a way out on the other side. But maybe there wouldn't be.

I made my decision not a split second after I heard the scratching coming down the hole above me. I had to get out of this room before it came back down the hole. I didn't know if my body would even fit through the other tunnel but I was a skinny guy. And it was my only option.

I flicked open the zippo, lit it and crawled toward the hole. My arms went first and then I shimmied my shoulders through, the thickest part of my body. I pulled my chest and hips through next. It was a little bigger than I thought with rock on all sides. Likely naturally forming.

I pulled myself through the tight little tunnel inch by inch. In the places where I had enough room to lift my head, I saw the black walls of the tunnel reflected in the flicker of flame. And the endless darkness ahead of me, never-ending. In some places the tunnel got tighter, or opened up a little. But there was nothing else to see.

I could hear the creature in the room behind me, scratching at its nest. I mouthed the same words over and over again: *please don't let it come down the tunnel.* I kept crawling.

I felt my hair flick back from my forehead and a cool breeze on my face. I stopped crawling and in that instant the flame went out on the zippo. The scratching was farther behind me now, way back in the nesting chamber. It wasn't coming. As my eyes adjusted t the darkness, I noticed thin daylight coming from my right. As quietly as I could I relit the zippo to see where the breeze - and the light - was coming from.

It was another tunnel, one that bisected the one I was in. I shoved the zippo into that tunnel and my heart dropped. There was a muted gray light somewhere at the end of it but it was too narrow for me to crawl through. I had never felt more like crying. The tunnel wasn't a viable option. So I kept going.

It was an hour. Maybe more. I eventually had to put the zippo away because I was worried about using up all the fuel. The darkness was blinding. Thick. It felt like a blanket, but not one that comforted you. One the smothered you.

And then the worst happened. I pulled my chest through a narrow section of the cave tunnel, assuming it was like all the others and would open back up immediately. When it didn't, I couldn't even reach my zippo to see what I was dealing with. My hips were stuck between the rock walls. Even though I could leverage my knees against the side of the cave and pull back, my body wouldn't budge. I was stuck.

I could feel the panic washing over me. It was dark. Cold. I was pinned in a tunnel, a hundred feet underground. I was alone and it was still. Silent. Until it wasn't.

I heard the thing in the tunnel somewhere far behind me. I had to move. Even if I had to break my bones, I had to *move*. And so I did. I struggled and pushed and pulled. I grunted and screamed in pain when I felt muscle tear or bone flex unnaturally. There was no point in trying to hide my position from the animal. It was coming either way.

And finally, finally - for no reason I could figure out - my hips were suddenly through. I yelped in relief, completely numb to the pain and crawled forward quickly. Right over the lip of the tunnel and onto a floor a few feet down. It was another room.

Ignoring my body aches, I grabbed for the zippo in my pocket and flicked it open. This room wasn't much bigger than the last. There was no nest or hole in the ceiling. There were some stalagmites.

But those were tertiary facts that I didn't notice right away. The *first* thing I saw were the bones. Most were small, likely from rats or prairie dogs. Squirrels. The biggest skeleton I saw was maybe raccoon-sized.

I kicked a few bones out of the way and spun back around toward the hole. The thing was still coming. I held the zippo up and waited, but the tunnel had gone silent. The creature didn't emerge.

When I felt confident it wasn't coming, I started to catalogue the room more thoroughly. No nest in this chamber, just bones and some sticks from outside. There was another hole in the chamber, this too high up on the wall for me to reach. And even if I could, I could tell already it was too small to get my shoulders through. I was trapped in here.

I fell back against the wall and slid down it, setting the lighter on the floor in front of me. I dropped my head into my hands and began to cry. I was thirsty and hungry and fucking tired. And it was becoming more and more obvious that I was going to die down here.

I don't know how long I sat against the wall crying. I only know that I was still sobbing when I heard the thing in the room with me.

SCRATCH

I jerked my head up and stared. The light from the zippo didn't stretch into the corners and that's where the thing was sitting. I couldn't tell its shape any better from here, but its eyes were like twin beacons of green reflected back at me in the light of the flame.

It moved its head side to side. Then up and down. It was watching me. Curious about me. Probably wondering what I was and what I was doing in its lair, so far underground.

"I'm not here to hurt you, buddy." My voice sounded strange after using it only to scream for the last two days. "My name's Kevin. I'm nice. I won't eat you, you don't eat me. Cool?"

It continued to watch me. I leaned forward and pinched the lighter between my fingers, push- ing it forward to get a better look. I wanted to know what sort of animal I was deal- ing with. The thing kept watching me. With the added light I was able to barely make out that the creature wasn't standing. It was sitting. And it looked bigger than when I'd see it on the ceiling.

I swallowed. "Do you know how to get out of here?" I moved the lighter further away from me and my hand bumped into some of the bones on the floor.

The thing shrieked. Shrill and high and terrible. It echoed around the room and I slammed my hands over my ears. The zippo tipped over and went out. I reached for it, scrambling to find it amongst the bones. I could hear the crea- ture on the ceiling again. It was above me, still shriek- ing. It made its way overhead, toward the other hole. It continued to shriek as it disappeared down the new tunnel. How it fit, I could only guess.

My fingers touched cold metal and I snatched up the lighter and lit it. The chamber was empty. I stood up and walked back over to the tunnel I had come out of. My skin was scraped to shit, raw and bleeding in many places. My ribs were bruised, maybe even broken. Breathing was hard. I could only risk going back into the tunnel if I had no other option. And it looked like that was going to be the case.

I walked around the new room, kicking the bones on the floor. I'm not sure what I was looking for. Something sharp, a weapon perhaps. There was nothing but small, sharp bones. One of them would have to do if I couldn't find something bigger. I walked around one of the large stalagmites in the room. There were almost no bones on the other side, the area clear. Intrigued, I stepped closer - and immediately realized my mistake.

In an instant my body was again encased in a hole up to my ribcage. This time my arms were pinned to my sides. I let out a sob of despair and then only my eyes remained level with the edge of the hole. I screamed in frustration and fucking panic.

This hole was wider than the one on the surface. I was able to kick and thrash my lower body. I sunk further in, the edge of the hole now a few feet above my head, arms still pinned down. I continued to flail, angry, desperate. Scared. And suddenly I was in freefall again, but it lasted forever. I fell deeper and deeper, struggling to catch myself against the walls of the hole but the dirt just came loose and rained around me.

And then there was no more hole and I was falling into a big room. Falling, falling, so far I wondered if I would survive it. The first thing to hit was my right leg. The bone shot right through the skin of my shin, shredding it. The rest of my body, surprisingly, hit cold water. I was under for a moment. Not sure which way was up or if I cared. Drowning wouldn't be the worst of my options at this point.

I broke the surface and screamed at the pain in my leg. I was standing in chest high water and holding onto the rock at the edge of an underground stream. I could feel the water moving around me but I couldn't even tell in which direction. The lighter was gone. It was pitch black. I would never see anything ever again. No Mom, no shitty car. No friends. Not even light. Just this sprawling blackness that sunk into your skin and invaded all the empty places in your body down to the bone.

I shivered in the freezing water, runoff from somewhere. Remembering how thirsty I was, I lowered my mouth to the surface of the stream and drank giant throat-fulls of water until I vomited it up, and then drank the somehow-dirt-dry-tasting water again.

As my thirst waned and the shock receded, I began to feel pain   again. My leg was fucked. The only way I was ever getting out of here was by crawling.

...or floating.

Shit. The stream! The water had to be coming from the surface. Clinging to the rocky walls I pulled myself against the current until I found the source of the water. It was a wall and the stream was coming from underneath it. I reached under it with my arm and then my foot but I couldn't feel another air pocket. There could be one. Maybe 6 feet upstream. Maybe 30 feet. Maybe miles.

I was running out of the energy to scream or kick or otherwise express my frustration. So in- stead I simply tipped back and let the current pull me away from the wall. The creature wasn't here, even though I had fallen down one of its holes. It was just me and the water and the darkness and whatever air this chamber had left to give me.

As I let the current pull me along I began to hear a new sound - the sound of falling water. Fall- ing water that was coming up quickly.

I reached for the wall, but the rock was smooth. I couldn't find purchase. I began to panic. The sound got louder. And then my legs were suddenly sucked under another rock wall along with the water. I braced myself against the wall as the current tried desperately to pull me under the wall and down the waterfall I could hear on the other side. It was certain death. I could hear how far the water was falling. I could hear the drop. And even if the fall miraculously didn't kill me, I would end up even further underground.

No, I would hold myself against this wall until my arms gave out. My shoulders were already protesting. The water's drag on my open fracture was excruciating. But still I held on. I wouldn't die like this. I wouldn't.

Minutes, maybe hours. I stayed pinned to that wall, body screaming. It hurt. And the fall start- ed to sound not so bad. Maybe enticing. A quick death. The water would carry my body. Maybe eventually find its way above ground. Maybe people would know what happened to me. I didn't want to die here, in this cave. I didn't want it to be my tomb. I wanted to know my body saw daylight again.

I don't know how long I was there considering the fall. And I don't know when I first noticed *it*. It tickled my periph- eral at first. Teased my brain. Just a whisper of it. *Hope*.

It started with definition in the rock wall. Then I could see the wisps of wet hair in my eyes. The shape of the water as it split around a rock several feet away. *Light.* There was light in this cavern. It must have been night when I'd fallen here. Day had brought the light.

The second I was sure it wasn't some sort of illusion I pushed against the wall, using reserves of strength I didn't know I had to twist a little. The light was there. Coming from a tunnel, a hole I could reach. A hole I could fit through. If I could get out of the stream without being sucked under the wall, I could climb out. I could get to that hole. I could see the surface again.

It took almost everything. I was exhausted. I didn't have much left. But with the addition of light, I could now see the edges of the stream. I could see a place to climb out. I could see a small stalagmite to my left that I could use as a handhold. A way to pull myself toward the low edge.

Saying a prayer up to a God I didn't much believe in, I turned away from the wall and pushed off, knowing that if I missed that little stalagmite I would surely be sucked underneath the wall and flung off the waterfall on the other side. I felt my hand close around it and I kicked with my one good leg, until I could get my other hand around it, and then my arms. I stayed there, clinging to that rock while the water raged around me, trying to tear me away. Muscle exhaustion was returning. My body was shutting down. I had stopped shivering. I need to get out.

I turned and kicked off the rock. The edge wasn't far and pulling myself out of the water was easier than I thought. The rock was smooth and slippery. Once I was out of the stream, I again lay catching my breath, resting my body. I was hungry. And so tired. My eyes drifted closed. And stayed that way.

It should have been the cold or the pain, but it was actually a sound that woke me up. The screech of a bird, maybe. I turned my head. The light from the tunnel was softer now. Perhaps late afternoon. I had slept all day. I tested my body and found that very little strength had re- turned from my rest.

I rolled onto my stomach and dragged myself off the rock and into the dirt. Inch my inch I made my way to the hole in the wall. The tunnel to the surface. If it was a bird I had heard, the tunnel couldn't be that long. And if it wasn't the bird, it was the thing from above. And it was in the room.

I got closer and closer to the hole.

Please be a bird. Please tell me it was a bird.

But as I reached the opening of the tunnel and looked through, I knew it wasn't. The tunnel was too long to hear a bird from the surface. The creature was in here with me.

I pulled myself through the hole and into the tunnel. It was about the same length as the first one I had fallen through and had a steady incline. I knew I must be underneath the hill and the tunnel would spit me out at ground level. And if I could get out, I could live.

It was long, it was slow. I had to dig deep for the strength to crawl forward every time I pulled myself toward the light. So I didn't immediately notice the creature was in the tunnel with me. I didn't understand why it was following me.

Curiosity? Boredom? Was it territorial? It only ate small animals and it hadn't attacked me yet. I tried to concentrate on the light in front of me. *Keep moving.*

The creature kept its distance. It could have easily caught up to me, but it hung back. I didn't care. I was now only several yards away from the opening. I could smell grass. I could hear the wind. I dragged myself faster. I was using my last stores of energy. I could see the end. I knew as soon as I pulled myself through the other side, my body would give up. Pass out. But I wouldn't be underground anymore.

I was five feet from the hole. I could see trees. I heard the creature behind me scratching as it followed me. But I didn't care.

Four feet. I reached out a hand. Some of the long stalks of grass were blowing inside the tunnel from the edge. I reached for one to help pull me along...but my shoulder caught.

It was exactly then that I realized something. I had been too focused on the light. The end of the tunnel. I hadn't seen the tapered walls. The low ceiling at the end. My chest was lodged. One arm was pinned to my side, the other out in front of me reaching for the surface. I couldn't squirm. I couldn't roll. I couldn't kick or push or pull. I had no more energy. I had no room. I was entombed in this tunnel. Able to see the world, reach for it, but never rejoin it.

I would never escape the underground.

I watched the long grass wisp back and forth at the opening. Watched the shadows linger. Watched the light dying.

I whispered for help, that was all I had left. The stars came out. I could see those, too. I could see the world, just right there. But I could never be apart of it.

When the creature began to rip apart my jeans and then the flesh around my calves, I continued to watch the night sky. While he ate my legs and then the meat around my hips, still I reached for the world.

And when I finally drifted into death to the tune of crickets singing; I thought, at least I had that. I would never get out of the ground. But I could see the stars.

THE DRAYTON TRACKS INCIDENT

On the morning of February 12, 1963 a small town in North Dakota woke to a strange and unsettling phenomenon. Drayton, a quiet city with a population of only 800, was built in the early 1800s on the bank of the Red River where they received trade from Ontario, Canada. That morning, however, the river had brought something else down from Canada. Something that seemed quite sinister.

Fresh prints in the snow has appeared overnight. They came out of the Red River but they were unlike any animal tracks anyone there had ever seen. The tracks were shaped like oblong hooves, almost 10 inches long and 4 inches wide, with a stride of around 3 feet. A local game hunter analyzed the tracks and surmised the hoofed animal walked upright and based on the gait was about 6 feet tall. The creature was thought to be between 250 and 300 pounds.

The tracks started on the shore line of the river and the depressions continued across a road, through a frozen field and then over an 8 foot tall fence. And by over, I mean that they stopped on one side and started again on the other. The thing had jumped it, somehow. The tracks continued onto a farmer's property, were lost in her backyard pond, reappeared next the house and then, curiously, appeared on the roof of the house. The family that lived there reported no thumping or disturbances the night before. In fact, they claimed it had been quiet and serene, as snow-covered nights usually are. They had heard nothing.

The tracks reappeared in the yard at the front of the house and continued into town. It was a quiet night, a Tuesday, and no one had been out at that hour. No one, they would find, except for Jacob LaMere. Jacob had had a drunken fight with his lover the night before and she had kicked him out of their house. He had had no choice but to wander the cold streets for a few hours until she calmed down. His tracks were there, too, on George Street, and the next morning, shaken awake by his girlfriend, Jacob explained best he could what he had seen in town the night before.

It was midnight, or perhaps one, he thought. He was drunk, pissed off, and cold. He'd walked to the bar, Rally's, on George. It was closed since it was a weeknight, and most people had to work at the nearby sugar refinery the next day. Jacob had banged on the pub door for a few minutes, begging to be let in from the cold and served a pint. When no one answered, he turned around to leave.

Jacob says he saw someone in the street then, from a fair distance away. He assumed at first that it was a person, because the thing walked upright and was the height of a man. But as he continued to study it, with one eye closed and a hand on a pole for balance, Jacob thought maybe it wasn't a man. Maybe it was a strange animal. It was dark in color, and seemed to get taller as Jacob studied it, but then shrink back down, and then grow and straighten again. It would not stay one height.

The thing shook silently, as if it were erupting in laughter at him, but the only sound Jacob heard was a low moan, like the creak of a building in the wind, long and low. It didn't take a step toward him, but in Jacob grew a very innate and ancient sense of fear. He turned and hurried back to his home, falling asleep in the shed and wondering if the whole thing had been a drunken illusion.

The tracks continued through town and into the forest beyond. There, the tracks became confusing. They walked right up a tree, as if no gravity existed, and then back down. Sometimes they seemed to jump from one tree to another. The people of Drayton were very confused. Still, they were able to follow them to an old cabin at the edge of the woods. No one knew who lived there. In fact, no one in Drayton had even known there *was* a cabin in this area.

The door was open and the tracks were inside. They walked right up to a crib in the corner. It was an old crib, but dressed with new blankets and sheets. A recently mixed up bottle of baby formula lay in the corner. Other than the crib, and a low burning fire in the hearth, the rest of the house was abandoned. It looked as if someone had been keeping a baby here, hiding it from town. But there was no baby in the crib now.

The tracks then led away from the bassinet and out another door. They continued through the woods, this time direct and deliberate, to the banks of the Red River where they disappeared into the water. The tracks were never seen in Drayton again and no one found out who or what was being kept at the cabin.

But there are theories. One in particular, seems to have particular merit.

On the third anniversary of the tracks appearance, a note was found just outside of town. It was written by Elena Havert, who had been 19 at the time of the incident. It said simply:

I didn't mean it. I asked it to take him. But I didn't mean it.

Elena's body was nearby. She had drowned herself where the tracks had first appeared from the Red River.

The note was found at the cabin.

WHITEFALL

You ever look back at the end of a fight with someone you love and think "how did we get here?" It was almost 30 years ago and I don't remember how the argument with Melody started but I will always remember how it ended: with me, packing my stuff and her, crying in the bathroom. If I had to guess, it was probably about money. We were in our early 20's. Neither of us had much family. Shit jobs, shit apartment, shit life. But we had each other. Loved each other. They told me that would be enough but, fuck, it wasn't even close to enough.

Three days of not talking to each other. Avoiding each other. I don't even think either of us were mad anymore, just...tired. Too tired to push the wall down this time. And then I got a call from my aunt and uncle in Washington. Come to

Thanksgiving. Work with my uncles through the holidays. They needed help on their tree farm.

I didn't even think about it, I just said yes. When I told Melody, I could tell she knew what I was really saying to her. Something my aunt and uncle didn't even know. I was going to Spokane for Thanksgiving and I wasn't coming back afterward. Melody didn't fight it. She just went numb. Like me.

I spent $42 on a bus ticket from Buchanan to Spokane which left me with $22 for food to eat on the three day trip. Leaving Mel, I was tired just thinking about it. My heart felt scalding hot, the one way ticket in my pocket as heavy as steel, pulling me down. But my bags were packed and I was here at the bus terminal.

The station was shit, as most bus stations were. No cell phones back then. No TVs. Just a smattering of humanity lounging in hard plastic chairs waiting for their number to be called. I took a long drag off my camel then pulled out my ticket, looking for mine.

Kristopher Stikes
Bus 881
Buchanan, Virginia - Spokane, Washington Departs:
1:35pm

I glanced at the clock on the wall 1:18. My eyes slid to the door involuntarily. I wanted to leave this station, go home to Mel. Find her and tell her I was sorry and that I wasn't going anywhere. But a small piece of me, the stubborn piece, just kept me sitting there. We had done this dance again and again and again. It never worked. Love was a luxury the poor couldn't afford.

"Bus 881 to Columbus, Ohio is boarding at Bay 7. Please proceed to Bay 7 for bus 881."

Shit. No time to finish my cigarette. I smashed the butt into the nearest ashtray and stood up, my eyes going straight to the front door. What was I waiting for? The solution to our problems striding in, easy as pie? A sign? Courage to leave and go back to her? God, I wanted that. I *wish* I had that. Mel was everything to me. And not enough.

"You leavin'?" I turned toward the voice, a small woman with a smoke in one hand and a baby in the other. She gestured to my seat. I took one last look at the front door.

"All yours." I picked up my bag and headed toward Bay 7.

There were six people ahead of me but the driver was quick, taking bags and checking tickets.

"That all?" He asked, waving toward my backpack.

"Yep."

"Buddy, you know you're going all the way the other coast. Washington. It's on your ticket. You sure that's all you got?"

"Yep. I'll just keep it with me." The driver shrugged.

I headed toward the bus door, waiting in line to board. I wished for the 50th time I could have afforded a flight. Buchanan to Columbus to Indianapolis to Chicago to Minneapolis to Billings to Spokane with bus changes in Indianapolis and some place called Whitefall in North Dakota. It was gonna be a long fucking three days.

As the woman in front of me boarded I looked back toward the bus station again. This was it. I would never come back to Buchanan. It was done. It was over. We were over. And that felt so wrong. It was me and Melody, always. We struggled but we always came back to each other. Poverty was a prison, but we were in it together. And now I was escaping alone, leaving her behind the bars. I couldn't do this.

"Hey, you goin' or what?" The guy behind me was short, a lot older than me, and clearly travel weary. He also didn't smell the greatest, but that was par for the course on these buses. "Well? Come on, man, I just wanna sit down."

I coughed and readjusted the bag on my back. "Sorry." I turned back toward the door and stepped up onto the bus. My feelings were strong but not logical. I loved Melody but if I went back now everything would be the same. This was a chance for her, too.

I picked a seat near the front, so I could be first off for cigarette breaks. There was a window seat available, and I took it, hoping no one would sit beside me. I leaned my head against the window and watched the rest of the passengers board. Lots of men traveling alone, a few families and one girl who couldn't be more than 18 or 19. She looked nervous and like me, kept glancing back at the bus station. Did she have reservations about leaving Buchanan, too?

The longer I watched her, the more certain I became that it was actually the opposite. She was nervous alright, but it seemed like she couldn't *wait* to get on the bus. My guess was that she was running from someone. Her eyes slid to the bus station and back so often it was almost funny. She hopped foot to foot and inched closer to the bus door every second as the driver checked her ticket and took her bag. I was watching her close enough that I saw the little sum she made when someone came through the door. I noticed the movement in my periphery, someone bolting toward our bus.

I sat up, ready to go out there and intervene if things got violent between the girl and whoever was after her. But when I turned toward the threat, I recognized that long, curly brown hair, heart-shaped face, and wild, green eyes immediately.

I tripped over seats and legs in my desperation to get off the bus. As soon as I stepped down onto the pavement, Mel was there, throwing her arms around me, her slight body wracked with great, heaving sobs.

"Kris, I'm sorry, I'm sorry. I thought I missed you. I thought you were gone and I wouldn't get to tell you."

"Mel. Mel, calm down, it's alright. Shh. It's fine, I'm right here."

"Kris..."

"I'm right here. I'm always right here."

I ran my fingers through her long hair, letting the curls wrap around my fingers as I had done a million times before.

"I-I thought I'd missed you."

"You didn't miss me, baby."

"You aren't coming back, Kris," she sobbed.

I had nothing to say. Because I didn't know what I was doing. Or even why anymore.

"I was gonna let you go. I was. I knew it was what you wanted and you were dying in Buchanan. Suffocating. I was gonna let you go and never come back, I swear."

"What? What's happening, Mel?" I whispered into her hair.

The driver slammed the door of the luggage compartment and walked around us, boarding the bus. "Two minutes, Romeo, and we're out of here."

"Mel. Baby, what's happening?" I asked again.

"I'm sorry, I'm so sorry. I didn't know. It was an accident. I just, I was sick over us, and I wasn't sleeping or eating, but I was still throwing up. Throwing up all the time. So I- I- I checked. I went to the dollar store and I checked. And I'm- I'm pregnant, Kris."

My hand froze in her hair for a few seconds. Pregnant. Mel was pregnant. My sign from the door. My baby. My girl. "Ah, Mel."

"I'm so sorry, I just, I thought you should know." She whispered. I hugged her tighter and breathed into her neck. I was an idiot. I could never give Mel up and even trying proved how much of a fool I was. She was mine. *They* were mine.

"Shh, it's gonna be okay. I'll make it okay. This is our baby. Our family. I should never have left, Mel."

"I hate this for you. I know you- you wanted a new start somewhere else." "No. There's no new start without you."

"Listen, buddy, we gotta go," the driver yelled down from his seat. "Kiss your girl goodbye."

I pulled back from Mel, running my hand along the side of her face. "Actually, I'm not going. I just need to grab my bag."

"No!" Mel shouted, pulling away from me. "No, you should go. Go be with your family." My face tightened, pulling into a frown. "I'm not leaving you, especially now."

"Make your mind up, kid, I ain't missin' my connection for this shit!" I recognized that voice as the travel-weary fucker that had been behind me in line.

My eyes went back to the bus driver above me. "You can go."

"No! No." Mel pulled my face down to look at her. "You wanted a new start in Spokane. Well.. well, so do I. You have family there. I'll- I'll keep working here and when I can afford a ticket I'll come to you."

"Fuck no. I'm not leaving you alone and pregnant in our shit apartment in our shit neighborhood."

"I'll be fine. I want this for you. For us. Kris, I don't wanna stay here either. I hate Buchanan. You were always the best thing about it. And I have a piece of you with me," she touched her belly and my hand went to cover hers. "I'm still staying with Mandy. It's safe. It's cheaper. I'm fine on the couch for a few weeks. Fuck the apartment. Go to Spokane. Work with your uncles. I'll keep working at Freddy's for awhile, save money, buy a ticket, and follow you."

"No."

"Kris!" She pulled me closer and closed her hands around the sides of my face. "I don't want to raise our baby here. Not here." She looked close to crying. She was right. *Buchanan* was the prison, poverty was the bars. I didn't want to raise our family here, either.

I took a deep breath.

"Let's go, Romeo, last call!"

"I will call you every day when we stop."

"Yes," she whispered.

"And every night in Spokane."

She nodded, trying to blink away the tears that ran down her face.

"Three weeks. You'll be in Spokane in no more than three weeks or I'm coming back."

She threw her arms around me and hugged me tight. "You know Mandy's number. I love you, Kris."

I hugged her back. "I love you, too. Both of you. Everything is going to be okay."

"Fuck, kid! Let's go!" The travel-weary fuck. Only this time his voice was joined by the agreeing moans of the other passengers.

"You'll call everyday?" Mel whispered.

"Everyday, baby." I kissed her head and then pulled back, squeezing her hand one more time before letting go. "Three weeks."

Mel nodded and then smiled for the first time in...I don't know. I remember when Mel used to smile. It felt like years ago. I forgot how beautiful it was. Like pure light.

I bounced up the stairs, hopped over legs, and jumped into my (thankfully still empty) seat. Then I turned to look at my gorgeous girl out the window. She was still smiling, though it was less brilliant and more warm, content. And that's how I felt, too. Fulfilled. Like no matter what everything was going to be alright. Because I was going to make sure it was. And *nothing* was going to stop me from taking care of my girl.

"Fucking finally," someone mumbled nearby. The driver shifted into gear and with a stutter the bus began to pull away from the station. Mel waved to me. She was still crying, but she seemed at peace. Because she believed in me. We were going to make sure everything was okay.

I watched her until we turned onto 19th Street. The bus station and my girl disappeared around a corner but I continued to look backward because I could still feel her there. I wasn't leaving her behind. We were a team.

"We're 11 minutes behind, you know."

"What?" I jerked forward at the voice. It was the Weary Traveler, sitting up in his seat and looking over the back of it. I finally gave him a good, hard once over. He was grizzled from the road but well-kept. He had to be in his 60's. The man's hair was an interesting spatter of brown and grey and his clothes screamed blue collar tradesman. His brown eyes were focused on me, narrowed and unhappy.

"We're not 11 minutes behind because of me. I held up the bus for maybe 5. Sorry." "I got a connection to make. I better not fucking miss it because of you."

I laughed. "I'm sure we'll make up 11 minutes by the time we get to your connection."

"You better fucking hope so. I'm going to Post Falls to see family."

I just stared at him, wondering why he was volunteering this information.

"That's in Idaho."

"I know where Post Falls is, man, I just don't care."

The man shook his head. "Little shit." He dropped back into his seat.

I leaned my head against the headrest and stared out the window, watching Buchanan slip away. The last twenty minutes had left me with a lot to process. I was going to need to convince my cousin Lloyd to take me on fulltime, not just through the holidays. I was going to have to work hard. Save money. That meant no drinking but I should probably cut that out anyway since I had a baby on the way. A baby. Holy shit. Mel and I were going to be parents.

"Good afternoon, everyone, my name is Bradley and I'll be your driver all the way up to St. Louis, if you're going that far. Our first stop is going to be Columbus, Ohio where those of you going to Pittsburg, Cleveland, and Louisville will make bus changes. That should be in about 6 and a half-"

I slung my headphones over my head and pressed play on my walkman, closing my eyes as the sweet notes of Guns N Roses 'Patience' drifted in. It was Mel and I's song.

"Hey. Hey, wake up. We're stopped."

I jerked awake, folding upright in my seat. The Weary Traveler was giving me a dirty look.

"Everybody has to get off. You're holding us up again."

"Fuck." I leaned forward and dragged my hands down my face wondering how long I'd been out. "Where are we?"

"Charleston. Come on, get the fuck off the bus so the driver can lock it. He needs to take his break." The man grabbed my arm and began to pull me out of my seat.

"Get off me, I'm going!" I shook him off and stepped out into the aisle, grabbing my bag and slinging it over my shoulder. "Not trying to hold you up, goddamn."

"Yeah, well you are. I have to make my connection."

"Me too, man. We've all got places to be." I climbed down off the bus and nodded at the driver. We were in a Mc-Donalds parking lot. Fucking thank god. I could take down half a dozen big macs right now. Now that I had my girl back, my appetite was, too. I started walking toward the door, already tasting those amazing burgers. But then I thought about how I

144

only had 22 dollars to eat for 3 days. Plus, I wanted to call Mel everyday. That would be long distance. And I wanted to talk to her for more than a few minutes... Maybe I should wait to eat until we got to Columbus. The bus station would probably have cheaper food like vending machines. It wasn't ideal, but it would get me through.

I pivoted and walked over toward a crowd of smokers standing against a wall. I had nine cigarettes left and I knew I couldn't afford to buy another pack on the road. So this would be it. Probably for the best, with a baby on the way and everything. Fuck. A baby.

"Excuse me." I turned at the voice and looked down at a girl from my bus. She was the nervous one, the runner. She didn't seem to be any more relaxed, but then again we were only a few hours away from Buchanan. Not far enough for her comfort, I'm sure. She was pretty, dark eyes and skin. Long hair. And though she was clearly on edge there was a directness to her. A strength.

"Um, I don't have any money to spare that I can give you but I was wondering if I could bum a cigarette?"

I shook one loose and held the pack out to her. She took it with thin fingers. "Thank you."

"Got a light?" I asked her.

She shook her head. "I don't have much at all, really."

I lit it for her and then lit mine. "So, where you headed?"

She took a drag off her cigarette and looked away.

"Playing it close to the chest, that's smart. You got a name?"

"Yeah. You got one?"

I laughed. This girl was gonna be just fine. "Fair enough."

"Well, thanks for the cigarette. I usually only smoke when I drink but-"

"Aren't you a little young to be drinking?" I smirked.

Instead of laughing or responding to my bullshit, she looked away again. The wind tried to carry her voice away but I heard her words anyway. "I'm a little young for a lot of things."

Fuck. I shouldn't have tried to tease her. This girl was not in a place for that. I cleared my throat. "Here."

She turned back toward means frowned at my out-stretched hand. "No."

"Here, take 'em." I shook the pack of cigarettes at her again.

"What...what do you want for them?"

"Nothing. They're yours."

She continued to eye the pack warily.

"I promise. Look I just, I just found out I'm going to be a father in like...I don't 8 months or something. I want to quit anyway."

Her eyes jerked up to mine. "The girl at the station."
"Yeah, that's my girlfriend."

The girls eyes drifted back down to the cigarettes. I sighed. "Her name is Mel."

That seemed to be enough, just giving this girl that much of me. She nodded, eyes still leery, and cautiously took the cigarettes out of my hands.

"Thanks." She pocketed the smokes in a ragged bag slung across her chest. We exchanged no more words. The driver eventually climbed back onto the bus and people began boarding. This was my last cigarette. Ever, if I was strong enough. Fuck, I just wanted to enjoy it. Savor it. But that meant I was the last person to board the bus. Again.

Weary Traveler took exception. As I dropped into my seat he shook his head at me. "Of course. You've got no respect for other people, son."

"Fuck off," I mumbled at him.

He shot out of his seat. "What the fuck did you just say to me?"

Louder: "I said, fuck off."

He grabbed me by the jacket and shook me twice. For a small guy, he was stronger than he looked and my knees banged against the metal chair supports. I grabbed his wrists and squeezed, pushing back. "Get the fuck off me!"

"You entitled little piece of shit, you've made the entire bus wait for you three fucking times and you've only been on this goddamn thing for four hours."

"Hey!" I heard the driver shout.

"Let go, you crazy fuck." I hissed at him, shoving him back   while trying to avoid the other passengers sitting in aisle seats.

"If I miss my connection I will punch your fucking lights out. I've got people waiting for me!"

"Hey! Knock it off right now and sit down!" The driver yelled again. No one was intervening.

"Look, I apologized for what happened in Buchanan. But last time I fell asleep and I'm goddamn sure I'm not gonna apologize for that."

"Just now you held up the whole goddamn bus to smoke a cigarette!"

"I got on the bus right after that family sitting in the back. *You're* the one holding the bus up right now, you sonofabitch."

"Sit down immediately or you're both being kicked off the bus." This time, the driver stood. Weary Traveler released me instantly and shoved me back. I fell into my seat.

"You crazy asshole," I mumbled. He gave me a disgusted look and sat back down in his seat in front of me.

The driver glared at us both. "If I see anything like that again, you will both be left on the side of the road. You're scaring people. There's kids on this bus. Do you got that?"

I saluted him with two fingers and the fucker in front just grunted something agreeable. The driver nodded. "That's your only warning." He sat down and put the bus in gear, finally pulling out of the parking lot.

I tried to fall back asleep but I was too hungry, too agitated. I stared out the window at the passing cars. Some had babies and I studied those intently. A little sedan went by, a father with his toddler in a carseat behind him. He was smoking a cigarette while his baby slept in the backseat. And even though the window was cracked I could see the clouds of smoke drifting back from the front to his sleeping kid. Hell no. That would never be me. I was done with cigarettes. I wouldn't be like that dad.

More cars passed us. I started to make up stories about who they were and where they were going. The Lincoln: New York to oversee a company merger. The pickup with the trailer: Louisville to buy a horse. The minivan with the smiling parents: Disneyland on a family vacation. Yeah, I would do that, too.

Take my kid to Disneyland. It was something neither Mel nor I had ever gotten to do. And, yeah, I wanted to do that for her, too.

"M&Ms?" I whipped my head around as someone dropped into the seat next to me. It was the runaway.

I was confused. "What about 'em?"

She frowned. "Do you want some?" She held out a yellow bag. "Sorry they're peanut, they were the only ones I could grab when I was... when I left." She trailed off and then looked down at the bag. "So, do you want some?"

I held my hand out. "Hell yeah, I'm starving. Peanut M&Ms are the shit."

She smiled then. It was small one, one that didn't reach her eyes, one that was more of relief than happiness but there is was. And like my Mel's smile, it was fucking beautiful. She tipped the bag into my waiting hand and didn't stop until the bag was empty.

"Are you sure? Because I got no issue eating all of these but they're your M&Ms."

She nodded and then crumpled up the wrapper, shoving it into her big bag. "I'm sure." She stood up and looked toward her seat at the back of the bus.

"Thanks." I said as I shoved M&Ms into my mouth by the dozen.

She looked back down at me. "You're welcome." Then she leaned down a little and lowered her voice to a whisper. "Maybe go easy on him, though, okay?" She nodded to the seat in front of me.

"Oh come on, you're on his side?" I whispered back, mouth full of chocolate.

She shook her head. "No. I just don't think he's trying to be mean. I'm pretty good at reading people's intentions. I think he's just anxious."

"Anxious about what?! He said he's going to visit family."

"I don't know," she shrugged. "Ask him." Then got up and moved back to her seat. I rolled my eyes. I wouldn't be asking him shit. With any luck he'd be boarding a different bus in Indianapolis. I wasn't quite sure where Post Falls, Idaho was but I hoped to God it wasn't by way of Chicago.

Night came slowly, the gray asphalt whizzing by outside fading to black and the cars alongside the bus darkening to unrecognizable colors. I could see city lights ahead of us, not warm and welcoming, but bright and sharp. Columbus. I could find something in the vending machine here. Fill up my water bottle from the fountain. Smoke a cigarette. Well, fuck, scratch that last one. I could already feel the inch until my skin. But I ignored it. Food. Water. Bathroom. Call Mel. These were the things I was focused on.

The bus took an exit and continued down several busy downtown streets before pulling up at the Columbus Bus Station. The doors opened and I stood to stretch, glaring at the clock in the front of the bus. I smiled. A few minutes early. Fuck Weary Traveler.

"Alright folks, everyone will have to disembark here, please do not leave any personal items on the bus. If you are continuing on Bus 881 to Indianapolis we will be boarding at 8:25. If you're continuing on to other destinations it has been a pleasure traveling with you and thank you for riding with us."

My first stop was the bathroom, then the water fountain and then the vending machine. I bought a pack of strawberry pop tarts and a bag of nuts, then sat down to eat. By 8 I was antsy to talk to Mel. I found a payphone in the corner and spent the 25 cents to call her. The line connected immediately.

"Hello?" I was disappointed when I heard Mandy's voice through the line.

"Hey, Mandy, it's Kris. Can I talk to Mel?"

"Hey Kris. She's actually working right now, pulling a double. She said if you called to tell you she'll be home around 2 in the morning."

"Goddamn it."

Mandy's voice grew soft. "I know. And I'm sorry, I tried to charge her nothing for rent so she could save more money but she said no, she'll pay. I have a feeling she'll be working as many doubles as she can."

"Is that..is that okay? Being on your feet so much when you're..." I didn't know what Mel had told Mandy

"Pregnant?" Mandy laughed. "She'll be okay. Our girl is strong."

"Right. Thanks, Mandy. Tell her I wont be able to call her until tomorrow morning. And tell her...tell her I'm right here. Can you?"

"Yeah, I'll tell her Kris."

"Thanks. Bye, Mandy." I hung up, grateful I hadn't wasted more than a quarter on a call where I couldn't even talk to my girl. I noticed there was a line at Door 9 for Bus 881. I wanted another window seat so I got behind a tall, lanky guy around my age. He hadn't been on the bus from Buchanan, but there were a lot of new faces. A lot of old ones, too, including Runaway and, to my immense disappointment, Weary Traveler.

I boarded after lanky guy and ended up across from him, in a window seat. As I flipped my GnR tape to the other side, I noticed Lanky Guy take out a notebook and start sketching. Or maybe doodling. It was hard to tell. I watched his hand move quickly and deliberately over the page. He must be one hell of an artist. There was no hesitation in his movements.

"It's a landscape. A mountain range."

"Huh?" I'd been so focused watching his hands I hadn't even realized he'd caught me staring.

His eyes shot up to mine briefly. "My girl likes mountains."

I nodded. "Cool man. You going to see your girl?"

"Yep."

"Cool." And that was it. Lanky kept sketching and I relaxed back into my seat. Only a few hours to Indianapolis and I'd be changing busses. Hopefully I could stay out of

Weary Traveler's way. I smiled, noting I'd been on the bus before him this time. He was near the back, with Runaway about halfway between us. I drifted asleep quickly, hoping I'd stay sleep until we stopped again at midnight.

"Hey." I jerked awake at Lanky's voice.

"What?" I said, my voice raspy.

"You dropped your shit."

My bag was on the floor, shit spilling out of it. "Fuck." I bent over and started shoving stuff back in.

"You sleep heavy."

"I know."

"My girl sleeps heavy too." He smiled a little then, looking down at his drawing which appeared to be finished.

"Haven't seen her in awhile?" I guessed, sitting back up. I didn't always like to get into conversations on trans-continental bus rides, but Lanky seemed cool.

"Yeah, almost a year."

"What's her name?" I asked.

He hesitated. I understood that. I didn't give out personal details to strangers either. "Sarah." He said finally. "She's an accountant. Smart. Way smarter than me. She likes me anyway though."

"That's cool. My girl's way smarter than me, too. How long you been together?"

"About four years, off and on. I think this time is for real though."

"Yeah? Good for you, man."

"Thanks," he said, closing his notebook and shoving it in his bag. "Well, there's Indianapolis."

I turned to look out my window. We were definitely heading into a big city. I could use a stretch and a cigarette. I couldn't even think about anything else. I needed nicotine. Fuck. But then I remembered the dad with the smoke clouding around his baby in the car. No. Bathroom, water, bus change. There was no point in calling Mel. It was only a little after midnight.

We reached the station and I bought another pack of pop tarts for the morning time. I checked my ticket and saw I was boarding bus 950 at Door 1 in about ten minutes. People were lining up already, so of course I did too, again hoping Weary Traveler was on literally any other bus. But there he was in line, near the front. When he saw me he shook his head in disappointment. *Well, I don't like you either, buddy.*

Runaway and Lanky were also in my line. I was happy about these two. They were alright company. The driver checked our tickets and let us board. This time, I was near the back. Runaway was a few rows behind, Weary Traveler even further back and Lanky was closer to the front. I ended up without a seat partner again and smiled at my good luck.

After a few minutes the driver climbed on. She was pulling the door shut when we heard a loud bang on the glass. The woman frowned down at whoever it was and then re-opened the doors. She nodded politely at the guy who climbed the stairs. He smiled and shoved his ticket at her.

"You almost missed the bus. It's after departure." The driver, a woman in her late 40's, told him before smiling back. "Glad you made it."

"Yeah, I gotta make it to Chicago. I wouldn't miss my bus, baby." He said to her and I automatically hated his voice. It slithered over your skin like a wave of grease, clinging and sour.

"Alright, well why don't you take a seat." She said, clearly put off at being called 'baby' by some nut sack in his late 20's.

156

Or maybe younger, with a hard life behind him. The closer he came, the better I could see him. He was scraggly, jerky, itchy, and possible high on something. And he stank.

The guy moved toward the back of the bus, studying everyone in every seat as he did. I had a sick idea of what he was looking for. I spun around to look for Runaway. She was sitting alone with a nervous look on her face as he came closer. She was getting the same vibes we all were. And she was the only single woman on the bus.

It was clear as day when Scraggle noticed her. His eyes lit up and he moved a bit faster. I started to stand up, hoping to move back to the seat next to her but he was too close. I saw movement out of the corner of my eye and glanced back. Weary Traveler has moved up to sit next to her. He saw my intention and nodded at me. He had her covered. I looked back toward Scraggle who was now frowning. He, instead, took a seat directly behind her. Weary-Traveler and I exchanged a look that may as well have been a conversation. He would stay right next to her and I was there if he needed help. I fell back into my seat and saw Lanky eyeing the entire exchange. Scraggle wasn't very big but he was likely volatile and unpredictable. The more people to help manage the situation, the better.

The driver, Sandra she introduced herself as over the PA, got the bus on the road and headed out toward Chicago. I was looking forward to getting there. It would be early morning and I'd be able to call my girl, and then again in Minneapolis.

Things were quiet for most of the ride as other passengers slept. The only sounds on the bus were quiet talking, light snoring, and Lanky scribbling. I still kept my headphones off in case of trouble and trouble was what we eventually got. It was early, just sunrise, when I heard Runaway shout.

"Don't touch me!"

I spun around just in time to see Scraggle pull his hand back between the sheets. "You looked so peaceful sleeping there. Beautiful. Like a princess." I heard him murmur.

Weary Traveler was already turned around, in the guy's face. "You don't touch women who don't give you permission to touch them."

"Calm down, old man," Lanky smiled as he relaxed back in his seat. "I just brushed her hair out of her face."

"That's not all you touched!" Runaway hissed.

"Oh, you liked it, baby, I saw. You were still asleep and you *purred* for me."

"Fuck you!"

The curse was loud enough to wake most of the back of the bus. I stood up and nodded at Scraggle. "Maybe you should switch seats with me."

Scraggle sneered at me. "I'm good where I am."

"It wasn't a request. The seats in front of my row are empty so you should be able to keep your hands to yourself."

"Yeah? And what if she doesn't want me to keep my hands to myself?"

"Believe me, I do." Runaway spat.

Weary Traveler stood up and nodded in my direction. "I think you should go."

"No." Scraggle laughed.

"Then she can move up," I said, and held out my hand to Runaway. She squeezed by Weary Traveler and dropped into the seat next to me.

"Now leave that girl alone." A man from the back of the bus said into the silence.

"Pervert." Another woman said quietly, though we all heard it. Scraggle turned around.

"Who said that? Who the fuck said that?"

"Let it go, man, we're almost to Chicago." I told him.

"Yeah? Well I ain't gettin' off in Chicago. Are you? How about that fine piece of woman you got there, is she?"

"Shut the fuck up, boy." Weary Traveler said and Scraggle laughed. The PA suddenly boomed over us, waking the front of the bus, to let us know we were in Chicago and for those of us continuing on Bus 950 the bus would re-board within the hour. Not much time.

At this point I needed a cigarette - badly. I even thought of bumming one back off of Runaway, but I couldn't stop thinking about the dad in the car, his baby in the back. I could be strong. For Mel.

As soon as I was off the bus, I was shoving a quarter into a payphone. Mel picked up on the second ring. "Hey baby."

"Hey."

"Where are you?"

"Chicago. I know you just got to sleep a couple hours ago..." There was silence. "I'm sorry. I just needed to hear your voice."

"I needed to hear yours, too. I miss you."

"I miss you, too. How are you feeling?"

"Good. Tired. Lonely. But I'm glad you went. We need to do this."

I leaned against the pay phone. "I know. But I hate it."

"So do I. It's just a couple months…"

"Weeks, baby. It's weeks."

"PLEASE DEPOSIT 25 CENTS TO CONTINUE THIS CALL."

I quickly dug in my pocket looking for another quarter. Shit. Long distance on a payphone was a quarter a minute? Fuck.

"Kris?"

"Yeah?"

"It's okay, I'm gonna go back to sleep. Call me from Minnesota?"

I sighed. Of course she was tired. I couldn't keep her on the phone just to hear her voice.

"Yeah, baby, I'll call in a few hours." "Okay. I love you, Kris."
"Love you, too. Goodnight."

I hung up the handset and ran my hand through my hair. Shit. Walking over to the vending machine I paid for a water and another pack of poptarts. If I had to eat nothing but poptarts all the way to Washington, I would. Nothing would stop me from calling Mel everyday for as many minutes as she would talk to me.

"Passengers traveling on Bus 950 to Minneapolis, please line up at Bay 16."

I walked over to door 16 and was for once happy to see Weary Traveler in line. But unfortunately so was Runaway. And Scraggle a few people behind her.

"Hey Runaway!" I called. She looked around for a minute until she found me. "Why don't you come back here with me?" Runaway saw where I was looking and eyed Scraggle as she passed him. He made a rude gesture with his tongue and she looked away.

"That guy is disgusting." She said when she neared me

"I know. Thought we'd let him pick his seat first."

Runaway nodded. And then, "Thank you."

I stepped a little closer, but didn't touch her. "You're welcome."

Since we were at the back, there were only single seats left. Runaway, I was happy to see, sat next to Lanky. I ended up next to a woman who hadn't been on our bus before and looked like she'd been traveling for months. She gave me a weary nod and then looked out the window. I closed my eyes for the first time in hours.

It was somewhere near Madison that the trouble started. I woke up to yelling and looked back to see Lanky taking a punch, Weary Traveler trying to hold back Scraggle in the aisle, and Runaway practically standing in her seat trying to get the bus driver's attention.

"You ready to trade seats now, pussy?!" Scraggle punched Lanky in the stomach again, Weary Traveler not able to do much to hold him back.

"Fuck off!" Lanky hit back but it didn't slow down Scraggle.

Weary tried to wrestle him down in the aisle. "Sit back in your goodamn seat!"

Scraggle knocked him off easily, then turned around and kicked Weary, a man clearly on the other side of 60. The entire bus erupted in outrage, but no one seemed to want to intervene. Lanky tried to push him away from Runaway again but Scraggle took him down with one punch to the face.

"Yeah? Anybody else wanna some?" Scraggle sat down in Lanky's seat and stroked Runaway's leg as she tried to kick him off. "Come on, baby, you can sit right in my lap."

I was over my seat and down the aisle before he could yank her down on him. I grabbed Scraggle by his shirt and hauled him up. Weary was old, Lanky wasn't accustomed to taking a punch, but I did manual labor for a living. And got into a lot of bar fights. Even high as a kite, and freakishly strong, Scraggle had nothing on me.

I dragged him down the aisle as he yipped and cursed. A few passengers got in a kick or two as he was pulled between them.

"Where the fuck you taking me?!" Scraggle squealed.

"You're getting off the bus."

"The fuck I am, they attacked me first! I was just trying to talk friendly to that girl!"

"Yeah, looked real friendly."

Sandra, who must have caught some of the commotion, was already pulling the bus over.

"Get off me! Ma'am, ma'am? This man is assaulting me and I would like the police called." Scraggle choked as I dragged him down the stairs of the bus.

Sandra scoffed. "Looked more like you were harassing that poor girl and kicking an old man. I don't tolerate that sort of behavior on my bus. You're getting off here."

She opened the doors and I pushed him out. He landed on his feet and spun around quickly. "You can't fucking do this! I paid! I'm calling corporate! Bus 950! And you can't just leave me here, you have my bag!"

A backpack came flying out of the door behind me and landed in a dirty puddle further down the embankment.

"There's your fucking bag." Runaway said, and then turned and walked back to her seat.

"Safe travels." I smiled at him as the bus driver pulled the doors closed in front of me. I watched Scraggle try to chase the bus and we pulled away. Other passengers flicked him off or insulted him out the window. Some gave me high fives or nodded approvingly at me.

Runaway was helping Weary back to his seat and Lanky was already next to him. I pulled out some Kleenex that Mel had put in my backpack ages ago and offered it to them.

"He got you good, Lanky." I said.

Lanky laughed. "My name's Dillon."

"Dillon. I'm Kris."

"Mack," Weary interjected from next to Lanky. "I'm Mack. Nice to meet you, Kris. Thanks for stepping in."

"Yeah, I was getting my ass beat," Dillon laughed.

"Oh, you were not! That dude was just super methed out." Runaway chimed in. "And thank you. All you guys, I'm Gracie."

"Well, that was eventful. Hopefully some of you are getting off in Minni for good." I laughed.

"Nope, I'm going through to Idaho." Weary - now Mack - said.

"Casper, Wyoming." From Dillon.

Gracie hesitated. "Billings, Montana. I don't know anybody there but...I don't know. I heard it's a nice place."

I nodded. "Spokane for me. Looks like we're all in for the long haul."

"Here, sit." Mack nodded at me.

"Why?" I asked suspiciously.

"We need to clean that."

"Clean what?' I asked.

"He bit you in the arm." Gracie pointed.

I looked down at my arm. Fuck, he had. Broken skin too. I leaned my head back and closed my eyes. "Shit."

"Don't worry about it, I'm sure you're fine." "Yeah, he looked real clean," I rolled my eyes.

Dillon laughed and then poured hydrogen peroxide on my arm that he'd gotten from... god knows where.

I must have fallen asleep again because the next thing I knew Mack was gently nudging me. "Hey, you want some jerky?"

I blinked and sat up. "What?"

"Jerky. You look like you haven't eaten in days."

"He hasn't." I heard Gracie from across the aisle.

I sat up and rubbed my eyes, and then took the strip of dried meet from Mack. "Where are we?"

"The border." Gracie said.

"Which border?"

"We're almost in North Dakota." Gracie answered.

I shot up. "What happened to Minneapolis?!"

"You slept through it," Mack said. "Soundly. Said you were going through to Washington, didn't seem any reason to wake you."

"No reason? I was supposed to call my girl!"

"Well, you can call her from Whitefall," Gracie said. "That's a terminal, a lot of people are changing busses there. Mack and me are."

"Well how fucking far is Whitefall?" I asked, exasperated.

Dillon's arm came over the back of my seat and hugged the headrest. "Couple hours. But you really didn't miss anything. Payphone bank was crazy in Minneapolis. I was supposed to call my girl, Sarah. There wasn't time. Call in Whitefall."

"Jesus." I knocked my head back against the seat rest. Goddamn it. I didn't know what time Mel worked today. I was supposed to call her from Minnesota. What if she was worried about me? We couldn't get to Whitefall soon enough.

Mack shared his entire bag of jerky with me - silently - and I was grateful. Maybe he wasn't so back after all. Just had someplace to be - someplace important I'd guess.

The snow started just after we hit the border. First gentle flakes, then a flurry, and finally a full-on white out. I had no idea how the driver could even see through it. And even though Whitefall was only supposed to be about two hours or so from the border, it felt more like 5. It even seemed like the sun was setting by the time the PA came on. It wasn't until then that I even realized we had switched bus drivers in Minni.

"Folks, this is Richard your driver, we're pulling into the Whitefall station now. Looks like we've got a few other busses parked which is great for you folks making transfers, everything should move on schedule provided the weather cooperates which, as you can see, it's pretty nasty out there. This is gonna be a twenty minute stop. Ordinarily I would mention some of the fast food restaurants in town if you want something hot to eat but I don't recommend leaving the bus station in Whitefall, it's a real blizzard out there."

He was right, it was hard to see anything at all, in fact. Slowly the clean walls of the red brick bus station materialized out of the blinding white. It was a sizable terminal, though not quite as big as Indianapolis. The bus pulled to a stop and the doors opened.

"Please take everything with you off the bus, everyone must get off even if you are continuing on with us to Rapid City. We are going to re-board at 5:40, the current time is 5:20."

5:20. This was supposed to be an unhurried 3 hours stop for me but it seems I would only have ten minutes to find and board Bus 414. Was the weather *that* bad? Had we been going *that* slow? I stood up quickly, hoping to be one of the first people off.

"Nice meeting you all, good luck. Mack, we only got ten minutes before our bus leaves."

"I saw." He grumbled.

The bus station was madness. There had to be 70 people inside, including us and it wasn't as big on the inside as it had looked from the outside. Everyone was shouting, people were snapping at each other, a baby screamed bloody murder on the other side of the room, it was absolute chaos.

"What the hell..." I heard Mack beside me.

"Whatever, let's just figure out what door we need to be at."

The ticket window was empty of a station employee so I went to the board near the front of the room. I found Bus 414 but across from it - where the door number should be - there was nothing. It was blank. In fact...they were *all* blank.

"What the fuck is going on."

The guy who answered my question was standing underneath the board, leaning up against the wall. He had on a Chiefs t-shirt and looked like he'd just pulled up in his daddy's lexus. "Busses are canceled. All of them. Board has been like that since the first one rolled up this morning from Kansas City."

"Fuck that, I have a connection to make! I gotta get to Post Falls!" Mack was red-faced and heaving. He was *pissed*.

The stranger laughed but there was no humor in it. "Start walking then."

"You little shit." Mack yelled, and tried to take a step toward the other guy. I put an arm across his chest.

"Relax, Mack, he's just some guy having a bad day. Like the rest of us."

"Yeah, we've all got places to be, *Mack*. So PLAY NICE." The douchebag taunted.

He walked away and Mack shook my arm off. "'Play nice', fuck that guy! Are all the busses really canceled? I gotta get on the 414 to Post Falls. Someone is meeting me at 9pm. I told her 9pm. I can't be late. I promised."

Gracie appeared. "Shit. The 312 to Billings is cancelled, too."

I looked back at the board and sighed. "Doesn't look like any of us are going anywhere. Should we find someone to talk to?"

Gracie snorted. "I tried. There's not a station employee or driver to be found. I even tried knocking on the 'employees only' door and no one answered."

"Shit," Dillon had suddenly appeared beside us as well. "I gotta call Sarah."

"Yeah, I gotta use the phone, too." I said. "Mack?"

"No...no. I don't...I don't have her phone number. Just an address. And a letter wont make it in time."

"Shit." I said. "Yeah."

I patted Mack on the shoulder and then followed Dillon to the payphones. There were two and only one was free.

"You go ahead." He said. "Thanks, man."

The phone rang so long I didn't think Mel was going to answer. And when she did, the connection was pretty bad. I could hear about 70% of everything she said but that was it. I apologized for Minneapolis and she understood. I told her it looked like there'd be a delay getting to Spokane and that I was stuck in a blizzard in North Dakota.

"That sounds terrible. How bad is it?"

"Remember New York four years ago?"

"Oh my god."

"Honestly worse."

She said something then I didn't catch. I asked her to repeat it.

Distortion...distortion..."doctor"....*distortion...*"an appointment"...*distortion...*" maybe Monday."

"You have an appointment on Monday?"

Distortion..."Kris?"

"Mel?"

The phone disconnected. I stared at it a few seconds before pulling another quarter out of my pocket.

"Don't bother. You'll get the same shitty connection." Warned a tall, blonde woman next to me.

I kept digging. "Well I at least want to try," I mumbled.

"Save your money, son." A older man said from beside her. "She's right. The storm is interfering. Might as well wait until it calms down some."

I took a look outside but all I could see was white. "You think it'll calm down?"

"It better." The woman said. "I have to get to Chicago."

"Right. We just came from there." I said.

The man next to her nodded. "Minneapolis bus. Saw you come in." He stuck out his hand. "Name's John Pollock. This is my daughter Emily."

I shook it. "Kris Stikes." I held my hand out to Emily and she took it as well in a pretty crushing grip.

"Better settle in for the night, Stikes. Nobody's getting out of here until morning." She told me.

"Yeah? Who said that?"

"Came over the PA, while you were on the phone." John replied. I exchanged a look with Dillon. Not good. And *especially* not good for Mack.

"Nice meeting you," I said curtly before Dillon and I headed toward the last place we'd seen the weary, old traveler. We found him sitting down in a chair near the door we had come in from. Gracie was next to him, smoking a cigarette. God, I could use one of those right now.

"How you doin', Mack?"

"You talk to your girl?" He asked.

I shrugged. "Bad connection."

He looked over at Dillon. "And you? You get ahold of your girl?"

Dillon shook his head. "Didn't seem much of a point."

Mack nodded. "So we're all fucked."

I sat down across from him noticing for the first time most of the people on our bus were seated in this area too.

"What do we do now? Just wait?"

Gracie nodded. "Yep. We're stuck here until morning."

"Anybody want anything from a fast food place?" A man I recognized from our bus asked. "I'm gonna chance the storm, see if I can find a McDonalds nearby or something."

A few people raised their hands and handed him money. God knew it was tempting. But I needed to save as much money as possible for the payphones. I opted for a snickers bar from the vending machine instead.

I watched him walk to the front door of the station. He struggled with the wind and the door and in the end, all he left behind was a dusting of snow that escaped into the building when he left. I never knew his name. We never saw him again.

We all did our best to get comfortable in our chairs. The baby, wherever it was, stopped screaming around 9. Gracie, who was stretched out on the floor dropped off first, settled between me in a chair on her right and Dillon and Mack in chairs on her other side. The station quieted down and by 1am there were only whispers and wind to keep me company. I tried calling Mel again around 1:30 and I think I got Mandy but the distortion was so bad it was impossible to tell.

I finally feel asleep around 3am and didn't wake again until 8. People were up and moving around by then. The sun might have been out but there was no way to tell. An impossible amount of snow seemed to have fallen overnight and the windows were almost completely covered by the drifts. There had to be 7 feet of it out there. It was ludicrous.

"Hey, you."

I rubbed my eyes and then looked over at a vaguely familiar man. "Me?"

"Yeah, you. What's your name?"

"Stikes."

"Okay, Stikes, well that guy took my money last night for a burger and he never came back."

"Okay."

"Probably took all our cash and got a hotel for the night."

"Okay."

"Well? What are you gonna do about it?"

"What do you mean? I didn't give him any money."

"Yeah, but you're the guy who sorts problems. Like the meth-head on the bus. I got a problem, you gotta help me sort it."

"Look, man, I don't know where you got that idea, but I can't do anything about your money. If he went to a hotel, he'll be back this morning to board his bus. Take it up with him then."

I left the guy and headed to the bathroom. The line for the women's wrapped around the wall and that morning I couldn't have been happier to be a dude. The bathroom was blessedly silent and I reveled in that, too. I could feel an undercurrent of anxiety and distress everywhere. It washed the terminal from wall to wall. In here, I was happy to be removed from it, and alone.

"Good morning, folks," cracked the PA above me. "This is the stationmaster speaking on behalf of your drivers and the Greyloor Company. I'm sure you're all very eager to board your busses and get on the road to your destinations. We sympathize wholeheartedly our passengers, so we are disappointed to have to inform you that the storm is not predicted to let up until this evening."

I could hear groans, and curses, and even yelling from the other side of the door.

"Our vending machines are fully stocked with food and drink so we ask that you do not attempt to step outside as the winds are in the 65 mph range and visibility is zero. For your safety please do not attempt to leave the station."

"Fuck you!" I heard someone yell through the door.

This was bad. Real bad. There were a couple of vending machines on each wall, but hardly enough to feed 70 people for an entire extra day. The one I had used last night was already almost empty. I dried my hands and walked out the door, heading back to our group's section. As soon as I sat down, Gracie offered me a cigarette.

"I know you're stressed."

I nodded tiredly. "I am."

"Are you sure you don't want one?"

I eyed the pack hungrily. But then I thought of the man in the car. "Hell, I'll have one," Mack grumbled.

The rest of the day passed slowly. We talked about TV, movies, video games, places we visited, but nothing personal. I ate poptarts and goldfish from the vending machine. Tried to call Mel again and exchanged maybe 8 words I could understand with her.

By nightfall, things were dire. We had been waiting all day to hear about the storm and our busses but no one showed up at the ticket windows and no one addressed us over the loudspeaker.

Around 6 I watched the stranger in the Chiefs t-shirt bang on the employee door with a couple other guys. They tried pounding on it, they tried shouting, hell, they even tried kicking the door in, but nothing broke. It had now been over 24 hours that we had all been stranded here. The baby screamed from somewhere, a man fought with another over the last moonpie in the vending machine, frustrated people tried the phones.

"What do you think, Kris?" Dillon fell down into a chair next to me.

"I think this place has a breaking point and we're gonna hit it tomorrow night." "You give them that long?"

"If we don't hear something over the PA before then, yeah."

"What do you think they're doing back there?" Mack asked.

I shrugged. "Drinking coffee, sleeping on couches, laughing at us."

Mack looked out the window. "The storm doesn't look that bad."

I had to disagree.

Sleep came easier that night due to my sheer exhaustion. I slept from ten at night to eight in the morning and was only woken by shouting. A man was trying to leave the station and two people I recognized, the father and daughter I'd met two days before, were trying to stop him.

"I have to get out of here, I have money, I'll find the cops or the red cross or something. I'll send help!"

"Andy, no!" Emily Pollock yelled. "You'll die out there!

"I can't stay in here anymore. I can't."

"Andy, stop!" Emily yanked back on his arm as he tried for the door again. "We *need* you!"

"More importantly, son, it's not safe out there," her father chimed in.

"Oh, let him go." The stranger with the Chiefs t-shirt laughed. "He's an adult, he can decide what we wants."

"Stay out this, this has nothing to do with your people."
"My people?" He asked.

"We've been on a bus with him since Arizona," her father explained. "We're concerned for him. Focus on your Kansas City people!"

"I've been on a bus with all *these* people," Chief's shirt gestured to a large group in the corner, "but if any of them wanted to leave of their own free will I would let them."

Emily Pollock laughed. "That's because you don't fucking care. Now piss off you pretty, mama's boy."

"My name is Acker but thanks for the compliment, bitch."

"Hey!" John interjected. "There's no need for that."

"Well, looks like you're a daddy's girl, too."

"Go deal with your own group, Acker." She snapped and the man she'd been holding hostage took that moment to jerk away from her, throw open the door and bolt through it. I was on my feet in seconds.

"What the hell? How did he get through the drifts?"

Dillon was behind me as we ran over there. It was impossible. The snow was higher than the windows. He should have ran into a wall of snow.

I threw the door open and found myself looking at a long, narrow hallway of snow, so high on both sides, I could hardly see the top. The passage went on so long I thought I'd lost it until I spotted the dark figure of a man hurrying away.

I was pulled back and the door slammed in my face. Emily Pollock was there glaring at me. "You fucking idiot, it's bad enough he went out."

"Who carved that path?"

"Who cares? It goes nowhere. We sent a girl out last night to see if she could find help and she never came back."

"You sent someone out there?!" I asked, horrified. I address this question more to John, as he seemed the more rational of the two.

"I did not agree to that but the girl and my daughter did. She went out of her own volition."

"That's insane! You sent some poor girl out there?!" Mack hollered from my left. "She wont make it a hundred yards in this!"

"She knew the risks!" The younger Pollock snapped.

"But it went nowhere, and now we've lost someone we actually needed!"

"What do you mean 'needed'?" I asked her.

Emily clenched her jaw and stared at me. Her father just shook his head. Neither volunteered an answer.

"He was a nurse. She needed him." Acker shrugged from the periphery of the argument.

"Needed him for what? Someone's sick?"

Emily laughed. "Everyone is sick, or will be soon. This our 3rd day here with no contact with the outside world. The vending machines are practically empty. The women's bathroom has overflowed. The people who are supposed to get us out of here refuse to open the door. Or even speak to us. They don't care what happens out here. People haven't slept. The phones aren't working. If we don't find a way to leave or get help, we'll all starve."

I looked around the station. My bus had come in late evening two days before. As I studied the room I noticed that people seemed to have huddled into four groups - one of them being ours, the passengers from the Minneapolis bus.

"There has to be another nurse or doctor here." I said.

"Yeah? Well, why don't you ask around the Minneapolis group. Because we had no medical professionals on the Kansas City side," Acker said. "So if you have one, send them over."

"I'll ask around." I said carefully.

"You do that." Acker smiled and I had a feeling I was missing something. Mack pulled me back to our row of seats and sat me down.

"You ever read Lord of the Flies, son?" Mack asked.

"No."

"What's going on?" Gracie asked, flinging some book she was reading onto the seat next to her.

"Look around," Mack said. "Do you see how this station is divided?"

"Yes." I answered. "By random groups."

"Not random," Dillon chimed in. "By bus." Mack nodded and seemed relieved, as if the burden of knowledge was off of him.

"Over there, the guy with the Chiefs tshirt. That group was on the bus that came from Kansas City. And over there, that dad and daughter we met the first night, that whole group is from Denver."

"And what about that group?" Gracie asked, pointing to the largest group, all of whom sat against a wall on the far side of the terminal.

"Salt Lake City. I was talking to a woman from their group earlier. Went over to ask if anybody had a stamp. She was polite but basically told me to fuck off." Mack grumbled.

"Right. What does any of this matter?" I asked.

Mack slid his eyes to me. "It means that the situation is devolving into every man for himself. More accurately, every *camp* for themselves."

"I think we can assume the loudest ones are the self-appointed leaders." Dillon rolled his eyes.

"Right." Mack said. "The guy in the Chiefs tshirt - Acker - seems to speak for the KC group. That woman and her dad seem to run Denver. I'm gonna guess the woman who stood up when I approached the wall is speaking for Salt Lake City."

"That leaves us," Gracie said.

"Right. And that's obviously Kris." Dillon nudged me.

"Me? Why?"

Dillon shrugged. "After the methhead incident, it just seems natural." Mack seemed to agree and simply nodded at me.

"Fucking great."

*

Later that night I woke several people up cursing at the phone. I still called. Mel or Mandy still answered. But I could never make out a word they said. But I still called. Because she had to know I was always here. And I was trying.

I slammed the phone back onto the cradle after it disconnected for the 3rd time and reached into my pocket for more quarters. Since all I had left were bills I decided to break one in a vending machine. I should probably eat anyway, it had been an entire day since I'd had anything.

I went to my favorite, the one with strawberry poptarts. The vending machine was against SLC's wall. A woman sitting on the floor next to the machine narrowed her eyes at me as I approached.

"What?" I asked her.

"What are you getting?"

"Poptarts."

"How many?"

"Just a package. Why?" The tone of my voice was no longer   pleasant.

"Because I need to know."

"Lady, I'll be goddamned if I'm going to explain why I'm buying a fucking poptart."

She laughed then. It seemed to surprise her as well and was a pleasant sound. She stood up and stuck out her hand. "I'm Amanda Hughen. You're Minneapolis, right?"

"Kris Stikes." I said warily.

"Alright, Stikes, you in charge over there?"

"No one is in charge. We're all just waiting for our busses."

She didn't say anything for a moment, just eyed me instead. "Let me give you a word of advice. No one here is your friend."

"I got that."

"Not even me."

"No shit, I just met you."

She stared at me a moment longer and then shrugged and sat back down. "Enjoy your poptart, Stikes."

"Alright, Hughen."

I ate my poptart in silence and watched the room settle down for the night. People were more restless. The baby cried louder, and for longer. I could hear fucking crying. The whole situation was disintegrating. Maybe that's what Mack and Amanda Hughen and even Emily had been trying to tell me. Things were dire. Circle your wagons.

It seemed like an over-reaction and I went to sleep thinking so. Until I was awoken at 4 in the morning by glass breaking. I was out of my seat instantly, Mack, too. Some guy had just been bashed into a long, glass shadowbox on the wall and Acker and some other dude were screaming at him.

"Did you think we wouldn't see you? That we wouldn't have someone awake?" The other guy yelled in the dude's face. "You try to steal from us?"

"No, man, it's just a vending machine!" The now-bloodied guy stuttered as Acker held him in a chokehold.

"It's *our* vending machine. Use the one in *your* area."

"Ours only has soda in it!"

"So drink a fucking soda," Acker laughed and punched the guy in the face again right before I got there. I yanked Acker back and the guy dropped to the floor. All of Acker's group were suddenly out of their seats and surrounding us. The situation was getting out of hand. I felt Mack behind me and then Gracie and Dillon broke through the herd on my left.

I flung Acker against the wall. "What the fuck is wrong with you? The guy was just tryin' to eat!"

"Yeah," Acker straightened and pulled his cuffs down like nothing at all had just occurred. "He can get food from Denver's area."

"You heard him, there's no food there! It's just a vending machine, man!" "Really? Well then let him get food out of the one by your group."

"He can! No one would stop him."

"What about two days from now? Or three? Or a week? What about when there's barely any food left? Then would you let him?"

"Of course!"

"Then your group is totally fucked. Might as well let that 5 year old lead it." He laughed, and pointed at a kid and his mom who'd gotten on with us in Columbus.

"You're insane. It wont come to three days or a week. They can't leave us here that long."

"It's been four fucking days, Stikes. No one has come. No one over the PA. Take a look outside, the busses are *gone*. We're alone. We've been abandoned. Get that through your fucking head. Or don't. Hell, it makes things easier for Kansas City. You hear that, everyone? When you're hungry, make sure you use Minneapolis's vending machine. It's a free -for-all over there."

His group laughed and then seemed to melt back into their territory. Mack grabbed my arm and led me away. Again. I could hear Emily screaming at the bloodied guy in the hallway. She seemed pissed he'd gotten into it with Kansas City. I also caught Amanda's eye walking back toward our area. I could read what she was telling me in her eyes. *Now you know the way things are. Be smart.*

The next day seemed different. My eyes were open to the actual dynamics of the station, all the things that had been going on in the background while I ate my poptarts and pined away for Melody. Again, there was no PA announcement that day. And again, people tried to break down or disassemble the Employees Only door. The employee areas we could get to had already been raided. There was nothing useful.

That morning I asked Dillon to take everything out of our vending machines and stockpile it in the corner. When he said he didn't have enough money, I told him to break the fucking glass, which he did. Within an hour, the other groups followed suit, breaking into their vending machines as well.

I tried like hell to get to the quarters, but they were in a locked metal box. I just wanted them for the payphones, to hear the line connect, to listen to the static. To tell Mel I was always right here. But I couldn't get to them.

We didn't have a doctor or nurse in our group, but we did have a nursing student named Miles. He was able to calculate body weights and, with Mack's help, rationed all of our food individually. There were 12 of us. And we could last 18 days at minimum levels for survival. I hoped to God we didn't need that long. I could only hope the other groups were rationing their food as well. And if not, we had a schedule of "sentries", so that two people from our group were always awake and watching for trouble.

We melted snow for water. Tried to wash clothes. Everyone stunk, the whole station.

By the 5th day, the situation was critical. People cried all the time. Arguments, fist fights, yelling. I watched a woman from Denver shove a woman from Kansas City into the wall. It erupted into chaos on both sides. Kansas City came after Denver and soon dozens of people on from both groups were fighting, Kansas City having the clear advantage. I was halfway across the room when Acker finally intervened, calling his group back with a laugh and telling them to "play nice".

On the 6th day, we finally got news. The crackle of the PA after so long probably scared everyone in the building, but we hung on every word that came after.

"Good afternoon, folks, Stationmaster here, just wanted to give you a quick update. We still have quite a blizzard outside so we are not able to depart any busses at this time, however we are hoping the weather will clear in the next couple days. So sit back, grab a cup of coffee or tea if that is your thing, and settle in. Please also remember that it is very important that you do *not* leave the station for your own safety. Thanks, folks, and we'll let you know when we know something more."

The room, which had been quietly gasping and cursing during the announcement, became loud and chaotic when it ended. I felt the same. A few more days. *Days.* The delicate ecosystem of human suffering would not support days more of this.

"Fuck."

"Fuck is right." Is all Mack said, and then sat down to work on a document he had been writing for the last few days. He was often writing or erasing and rewriting. I knew better than to ask him about it, but Gracie seemed to think he *needed* to do it.

"I don't suppose you got anymore of those M&Ms, Gracie." I asked one day when I caught her counting out individual nuts for the rations.

"Fuck, I wish." She grumbled.

Most of the last couple days for me had been getting to know the other people in the Minneapolis group and playing cards. Gracie was the best at poker and often ended up with all the peanut shells, which we'd been using as chips. Mack played too, but seemed less and less his usual jovial (read the sarcasm there) self as the days passed. Dillon drew a lot and talked about Sarah. How he'd met her (work), why they'd broken up (his fear of commitment), when he realized he loved her (ran into her years later at a New Years Eve party), and how it was going to be different this time (which, he didn't have all worked out, but he had faith).

The following day was the 7th day, a milestone, an entire week. We all had horrible headaches from the ever alight, bright, florescent lights. We weren't eating as much as we should and we were all bored to tears.

This was the mood when Amanda and John Pollock approached us with two other Denver-ens in tow. The groups had all kept strictly to themselves since the night of the big fight between Denver and Kansas City so I was immediately wary.

I met them at the top of the aisle, with Mack and Dillon at my sides. "Pollocks. What can we do for you?"

John cleared his throat. "We are actually just taking stock of food. Our area had a cigarette machine and a soda machine, so we have run out of actual food fairly quickly. We were hoping-"

"We need all the groups to donate food to Denver," Amanda interrupted. "We're dying."

"You're dying?" I asked.

"Yes," she hissed. "Or we will if we don't get any food."

I shrugged. "What do you have to trade?"

"Are you kidding? This is a matter of life and death, you heartless fuck."

"Exactly," Dillon said. "So what do you have to trade?"

"We're not trading anything." Emily hissed.

"Pity," Gracie said, standing up on chair next to us. "You can't get something for nothing, you know."

"Cigarettes!" John said. "We can trade you cigarettes. And soda."

"Dad, no. They don't need any of that."

"We'll take it," I shrugged. "Keeping up morale is important, too. Cigarettes and soda will help."

"You got any weed?" Gracie asked as she leered over the exchange.

"Why don't you just give us some food and when you want a cigarette-" Emily started.

"No. We have 12 people to feed, including a kid. You have 15. You want food, you trade. And I'm guessing you really want food."

"Fine!" Emily snapped. "We will make a trade."

"One moment."

I walked back into the Minneapolis group and let them know what was happening. Most people were okay with a trade, as long as we got enough back, and as long as there was enough for us to survive for another week. The mother and her son were less enthusiastic about it, but as a parent, I wouldn't trade food my child could eat for soda and cigarettes either. But there were other people in this station who could starve if we didn't. I returned to the Pollocks with my offer.

"We want 20 sodas and 20 packs of cigarettes. We'll give you 15 packs of nuts, 5 packs of trail mix, and 10 assorted candy bars in trade."

"That's absurd!" Emily yelled. "We need more - we have 15 people!"

"Then I suggest you ration it." Mack responded.

Emily sneered and stepped up in Mack's face. I tensed, sure she was going to try something but all she did but stare and then tell him, "You stink." To which Mack laughed. All we'd been able to have were makeshift "showers" in the bathroom sinks. Everyone stunk.

We exchanged what was promised and then I watched as the Pollocks made a similar deal with Salt Lake. They had more people, so offered less but Emily kept her temper in check this time. Finally, I saw them make their way over to Kansas City. Before I could even wonder how that would go, Acker's voice carried across the entire building. "Keep walkin', honey, you don't have anything we want."

She said something back to him and Acker laughed. Hopefully whatever she got from us and Salt Lake would be enough to get by for a couple more days.

By the tenth day at Whitefall, no one was crying or screaming or fighting anymore. Most people slept a lot. Conversations were quietly spoken. I occasionally saw people quietly leave of the station when it was my turn for watch. They looked like they'd had enough. They never came back.

Salt Lake was the first to really struggle. They had the biggest group, but had still tried to share with Denver. They were down to half rations before any of the other groups. We offered them what we could spare. But still, on the 16th day a rumor spread that someone had died. I watched them haul the girl out into the snow. She was very slight to begin with, not an ounce of fat on her. Her skin looked gray. Amanda looked shell-shocked. I knew she felt responsible. The girl was hers, from the SLC group. I'll remember that look for the rest of my life.

By the 18th day, I realized the baby wasn't crying any-more. We were dangerously low on food. Miles had dropped us to half rations. I still called Mel just to hear the static. But I talked to her all the same. Told her how much I loved her, and our growing baby. Told her I was always right here.

The boredom had really gotten to people. They laid around staring at walls, half catatonic. They begged Miles, keeper of our food, for something to eat. He'd just shake his head every time, not say anything. He looked to be cracking, too. Mack worked on his pages. Dillon drew. Gracie counted almonds over and over again. People played cards. We waited for rescue.

On day 19, we were awakened from our stupor by the loud cack of the PA again. It had been weeks and most of us were too shocked to react to the noise.

"Morning folks! Just wanted to give you another update. We've heard from the national weather service that the storm shouldn't let up for another ten to twelve days. Not what you wanted to hear, I'm sure. But chin up! Help yourself for a coffee or tea and please, of course, let us know if you need anything or have any concerns. We can't wait to get you back on the road."

Dead silence reigned after the PA shut off. Shocked silence. Appalled silence. Until some guy from Denver broke it.

"I have some fucking concerns!" He screamed, and ran full force at the Employees Only door, using his head as a battering ram, again and again. I could see the blood spreading across the metal door from across the room. People sprung up out of their seats, but not to help him. No, they flung him aside and began battering the door. Over and over, piles of people, running into the door, shoving against it again and again. I could hear the metal buckling from the other side of the room. I was honestly surprised people had the strength after eating so little but then I noticed most of those battering the door were Kansas City. They hadn't shared any of their rations with the other groups.

A loud crack and the door broke in. People trampled each other to get inside, and Mack and I were hauling ass over there immediately as well. "Grab what you can!" I yelled to the rest of the group, who followed us in.

Beyond the door was fucking anarchy. People grabbing and tearing at everything, from coffee grounds for the staff coffeepot to rolls of paper towels to books. I could only hope my group was hoarding shit as well.

The inside of the room was pretty disappointing in the end. A carpeted room with lockers, a couch, and a few nicer chairs and another, smaller room with manifests, route maps, and the PA system.

"Where the fuck are they?" Dillon yelled. Where indeed. There were no drivers here. No one to make the announcement. There was nothing. No one. So where had they gone? Where was the man who had been speaking to us five minutes ago?

I became aware of a commotion at the same moment that Mack tried to clue me into it. Acker and a couple others of his group trying to push people out.

"What the fuck, Acker? This ain't your show." I said, coming into the main room. He turned to me and spat on the floor at my feet.

"This is Kansas City territory. This room, and everything in it, is ours."

"Fuck you, that is not happening!" Gracie said, and then picked up an empty coffee pot and hurled it at the wall.

"Now, now, play nice, little girl." Acker purred at her.

"Hey," I snapped my fingers in his face to get his attention back on me. "You think you own this room because the door is near your so-called territory?"

"Yeah. But if you want to dispute that, we'll gladly reconsider."

I didn't need to look around the room to know that would never happen. Acker's group was surprisingly healthy looking and had more men than women or children. The other groups, even mine, were pale and tired. If he wanted carpet and a couch, he could have them.

"Books," I said. "Let us take as many books as we want and we wont dispute your claim to this room."

Some brunette standing next to Acker laugher. "Take the fucking books." "You got anyone knows radios in your group?" Mack asked him.

Acker narrowed his eyes at Mack as if debating if he should answer and then nodded tightly.

"Try to rig that PA system to call out. Or maybe look around for a system that will." Mack said.

"We don't want to be here any more than you do, old man." Acker said.

"Fine." I turned to my group. "Take the books, as many as you can handle. It'll help with the boredom. Yes, everything, take everything." I wasn't about to leave them a single fucking page.

Amanda Hughen seemed to agree and her group, bigger as it was, took even more than we did. I saw someone with a copy of The Shining and plucked it right out of their hands. "I'll take that one." Why not? It fit the mood.

"The Shining, huh?" Gracie said, noticing the book in my hand.

"Yep. Stephen King. Genius stuff. Something to pass the time since we only hear from the PA once a fucking month."

"Yeah. What I wanna know is where's this fucking coffee and tea?"

The groups kept to themselves for the rest of the day - Kansas City locked behind the Employee's Only door. I could only imagine what was going on in there. So far they hadn't fucked with anybody so I was happy to let them keep to themselves.

It was a couple days later, maybe 9 o'clock at night that the first murder occurred. Most of us were reading, a few of us sleeping. Gracie and Dillon were playing cards. I was in a conversation with Miles. The food, even at half rations, would only last a few more days. Things were dire. It was time to drop to quarter rations, like Salt Lake and Denver had days before.

"What about boiling clothes or leather or something?"

He shook his head. "We'll do it, but it's not gonna be enough."

"Fuck."

"Maybe we can talk to Kansas City."

"Why Kansas City?" I asked. "They're fucking danger-ous. Likely to stab me just for asking."

"Because...look at them. They're not weak. Not one per-son in that group is showing signs of malnutrition. They have food. Denver and SLC are as fucked as we are."

I sighed and looked toward their door. "Shit."

The word was hardly out of my mouth before the door was flung open and a guy from Denver was pushed through it. He was young, 20's maybe, and he was small.

"Pollock!" Acker followed the stumbling man out. "Where the fuck are you, woman!"

She emerged from the hallway her group had been us-ing, a bored look on her face."What is it? What are you doing with Jeremy?"

"You mean your little spy? We caught him creeping through a vent, trying to get into our area. You know anything about this?"

"Of course not." She spat. "Do you think I'm stupid?"

Jeremy, for his part, looked terrified. He said not a word, and tried to catch himself as Acker and the brunette - I think her name was Natalie - shoved him between them violently.

"You're saying you didn't send this little prick to steal from us?"

"No! We wouldn't do that! You have nothing we want. You forget, we've all been inside your little room."

Acker studied her a moment longer and then picked up Jeremy and shoved him at her feet. The rest of the KC group seemed to materialize behind her, looking healthy and strong, just as Miles had said.

"Then deal with him. In front of everyone here." He spread out his arms and gestured to the entire station. "Show us how you deal with thieving spies. Or we'll deal with you, since you seem to speak for Denver."

"I- I wasn't going to take anything-" Jeremy protested, but then Emily kicked him in the ribs and he gasped.

"Yeah," Acker smiled and leaned back against the wall folding his arms. "That's a good start."

Emily didn't even hesitate. She kicked him again. And then again. And because she was too weak to do any more damage, she addressed her group. "Participate in Jeremy's punishment, all of you."

A couple members of her groups stepped forward, also looking hesitant. The others stayed back. Emily stepped away and gestured at Jeremy again, who was moaning on the floor and bleeding from his mouth. "Participate or you don't eat today. Or tomorrow."

"Jesus." I mumbled and Mack who had appeared along side me agreed.

It was brutal. The kicks, the punches, they were weak. But Jeremy, like his attackers, was frail. It went on for an entire minute before I couldn't take it anymore.

"That's enough, Emily. You're going to kill him!" I yelled as I left my group to approach the chaos.

"Yes, that's quite enough," John Pollock agreed. "I would say he's learned his lesson. Everyone stop."

"No." Emily said quietly. But it didn't matter that the words were soft. Her group wouldn't have heard them anyway. They were mad with bloodlust, punching, kicking, angry. Angry at their situation, the hopelessness of it, their likely impending deaths. But not at Jeremy, who by now had gone silent. And when the last of them finally ran out of steam and collapsed on the floor next to him, Jeremy breathed his last death rattle.

"Oh my God," I heard Gracie whisper from somewhere behind me. Emily ordered the body dragged outside, KC went back into their room, SLC looked on as if nothing had happened, and I dropped into a seat next to Dillon, who continues to sketch mountains for his Sarah.

"Everything is going to be different now," he said without looking up from his book.

And he was right. That was the night the power went out. It had been over three weeks and we had all gotten used to the blinding, florescent lights, which never dimmed and always hummed. I didn't mind the darkness so much at first. We had lighters and someone had found a couple candles among the books in the employee break room.

It was heat we missed most and that became an issue within the first hour. I had everyone pull out all the clothes in their bags and then assigned them so that everyone in my group would stay as warm as possible. Next, we inventoried matches and lighters. When that was done, we dragged two metal garbage bins in our territory into our area, and piled all the wood we could find - chairs, small tables, wall paneling - into the corner of our section next to the food.

I watched as the other groups did the same. Salt Lake City and Minneapolis each had piles and piles of books which would work for kindling. Denver, as far as we could tell, only had a few books, or none at all. No one had any idea what was happening behind the closed door of KC's new territory. But it wasn't long before we saw the orange glow of a fire underneath the crack in the door. That made sense. They has years of paper manifests and charts back there. The smoke, with no where to go hovered over us. We had to crack the doors for ventilation, which only seemed to make it colder.

Time became confusing. Miles lost track of when to feed people. My watch kept running but the time never seemed right. Day bled to night and back to day slower than I thought it should have.

Life became a slow, boring, painful nightmare. We burned the books slowly, took turns in front of the fire. Denver struggled with their fire. They started eating snow, which Miles had already told me was one of the worst things you could do. It burns energy to warm snow up in your body. We tried to tell them but Emily told me to fuck off.

And then one day Amanda came to speak to me. I'd just hung up the phone - my hundredth call to Melody, to listen to the static and tell it that I was always there. I hadn't heard Melody's voice in weeks.

"Stikes."

I looked up to find the tall woman standing at the pay-phone next to me. She was pale and thin and her skin was purple in places. I imagined I looked much the same. I nodded at her.

"How you been?"

I shrugged. "Could be better, I guess."

"I know the feeling. Have you...lost anyone?"

I shook my head. "Not yet. But soon." Everything felt heavy in my chest. We would lose someone soon. An older woman name Valerie, or possibly even Mack, who was more absorbed in his letter-writing every day. People were starting to get sick.

"We lost someone last night."

"I'm sorry, Amanda. You have a bigger group. It was bound to happen to you first."

"Yeah...he got sick. Alex, he was, he was in his 30's, healthy, but he just got sick..."

"I'm sorry."

She took a deep breath. "When we went to bring him out to the snow, to bury him where we buried Andrea, she... she was gone."

"What do you mean. She wasn't dead?" "No, she was definitely dead."

My brain was cloudy, slow to work, slow to process. "Are you saying she got up and walked away?"

"No. I'm saying someone took her." "Someone took her body?"

"Yes, Stikes, someone took her body." "What for?"

"We don't know. But, you know Natalie from Kansas City?"

"Yeah, I know that cunt."

"Yeah. Well yesterday when she came out to use the bathroom, she was...she was wearing Andrea's jacket. The one we buried her in."

"Okay. So Kansas City stripped her corpse for clothes."

"I think there's more to it than that, Kris."

"You think they're...abusing her corpse?" I didn't know a politer way to say it.

"No. Stikes, come on. Think about it."

"They're eating her." I heard Gracie before I saw her. She had been standing next to me - for god knows how long.

"*Eating* her?"

"We think so too. Our wall is near their door. We smell...we smell meat cooking sometimes. Do you remember when they first moving into that room?"

"They were almost as starving as we were," Gracie answered.

"Right. And have you seen them lately?"

"Oh fuck," I groaned. This was something...this was wrong. Eating *dead bodies*.

"So what I'm saying is, be careful of Kansas City. Even more than you have been. Andrea is dead, Jeremy is dead, and now Alex. What's gonna happen when they run out of...supplies."

"I gotta talk to Mack." I ran a cold, numb hand through my greasy hair. "Listen, maybe we can agree to some sort of alliance. We'll watch your back, and you watch ours."

She nodded. "I think that's necessary at this point."

I nodded goodbye and then stalked over to Mack, who was viciously erasing a sentence from his letter. "We gotta talk."

"Oh yeah? About what?"

"Kansas City."

"What'd they do now?"

"Salt Lake thinks they're eating the dead."

Mack nodded and kept writing. "That makes sense."

"Mack, this is a big deal. They got the first girl that died, and that kid Jeremy. And Amanda lost someone last night, but he was sick. Not sure if they'll eat him."

"You're worried about what happens when they run out of meat stock."

I recoiled at his phrased. "Yeah. If that's what they're doing. They're stronger than we are."

"Yeah, well, we've got a bigger problem than that."

I leaned forward. "What problem?"

"I don't know if you've been watching but Denver don't have no fires today."

I threw up my hands. "We have enough to deal with trying protecting our own people and now Salt Lake, I can't be concerned with Denver getting cold!"

Mack stopped writing and flipped the page over. He looked up at me with hooded eyes. 'What do you mean 'now Salt Lake'. What did you promise them?"

"Just that we would watch their back and they would watch ours."

"Are you kidding me? We don't have the resources for that! Or the energy! They're a big group and their territory has a strategic disadvantage, especially for defense. That Hughen women means well but that group is *fucked*."

"They have huge numbers. We-"

"Huge numbers don't mean nothing if they can't even stand up!"

"What was I supposed to do, Mack? Huh? She didn't have to warn me about KC."

"Like I said, we've got bigger problems than some cannibalism."

"Bigger problems than some... Like what?"

"Like that fact that Acker and the Pollocks have been talking an awful lot lately."

"Fuck. Dillon!" Dillon was the most observant person I'd ever met. He was a good person to have in this conversation. "Come here!"

Dillon handed his notebook to Dan, the five year old in our group. Dan was pale and thin, definitely showing signs of malnutrition but he was also eating the best out of all of us, we made sure of it.

Dillon sat down next to Mack and nodded at the letter. "Get it right yet?" He asked.

"Getting there," Mack mumbled. "Not like she'll ever read it. Just passes the time." I was curious what he meant, who it was for, but like Mack said, we had bigger problems.

"What do you think about the Pollocks and Acker?"

Dillon shook his head. "I don't know. Looks kinda like they made a deal about something. Possibly food. More than likely a power alliance, though."

"That doesn't make any sense," Mack crossed his arms. "Denver is the weakest group. Acker couldn't have chosen worse."

"Not necessarily," Dillon answered. "Denver is also the most ruthless of the three of us."

"Which mean whatever deal they were trying to make, it was not good for us." I sighed. "Fuck."

Dillon shrugged. "We'll just have to wait and see."

"No. No we don't. We need something to defend ourselves with. The metal from the chairs or something. We can break them and bend them into big fucking metal pipes."

"If we have the energy, we can try," Mack nodded.

So we did. It was exhausting and what we got out of it may not have been worth the effort. The fruits of our labors were seven, jagged, sharp, curved pieces of shiny metal. It wasn't great, but it was better than nothing.

It could have been hours, or it could have been days later that the raid happened. By the time I was woken up, it was already over. Dillon and Jessica had been on watch and it seemed that was all they'd done.

"What happened?" I asked, looking over at the SLC group who looked scared and a little shell-shocked.

"Kansas City and Denver went over. Acker and the Pollocks exchanged some words with Amanda. It didn't seem to go well. Emily grabbed some girl from Salt Lake and shoved her head into the broken glass of the vending machine. She was bleeding... everywhere. Salt Lake is big, they tried to fight it but...they're just so weak. With KC backing them, the fight was quick, lots of injuring in Salt Lake. Denver and KC together... Kris, there was nothing we could have done. Even if you were awake."

"I promised them... Fuck. What did they take? Their food?"

"Their books." Dillon answered. And that was when I noticed that SLC didn't have a burn barrel for warmth. And Denver did.

"Shit. I'll go talk to Amanda."

She was curled on her side, laying against a wall. When I had met her weeks ago Amanda had been a confident, strong, vibrant woman. But now she looked like a different person entirely. I kneeled down next to her.

"I heard about what happened last night. I'm sorry."

"There's nothing you or your group could have done. Denver and KC together...we were too weak to fight it."

"We've got a decent supply of books. Why don't you come join our group. We'll figure out food and then at least you'll be warm-"

"I suggested that this morning, with what's left of SLC. They don't want anything to do with the other groups. Yours included."

"Amanda...they'll die. Do they realize that?"

"Yes. They're tired. We're all tired. No rescue is coming. They've accepted it. Before long, we'll all be eating each other."

"No. We won't."

She gave me a half smile that didn't reach her eyes. Then she closed them and coughed. Fuck. "I hope you survive this, Stikes."

*

I did survive it. But John Pollock didn't. Days later Kansas City came out of their room, something they rarely did anymore. They dragged a desk out behind them.

Dillon and I were at the payphones. Me, listening to the static, Dillon talking softly down the line, to Sarah, or whom he imagined was Sarah, I assume. There was very little to keep us sane after a month at Whitefall.

Acker, Natalie, and a few larger members of Kansas City approached Denver's hallway. John stepped out first, followed by his daughter Emily. The rest of Denver stayed back against the wall.

"So." Acker started. "Denver. What you provided us, that wasn't the deal."

Emily folded her arms, tried to appear casual but it was obvious from the sweat on her brow that she felt anything but. "Holding out on you how? You got what was promised."

Acker laughed. "Did I? Because it seems to me that while you got the books you begged for, *we* did not receive the payment you promised. So where is it?"

Emily shifted on her feet. "We delivered you the boy-"

"That was *not* the deal. You were very aware of the terms when we agreed to assist you in finding fuel for your fires. So, where. Is. The. Woman?"

Emily dropped her arms. "We're starving, too. There are 14 people in my group, we need to eat. We only had cigarettes and soda in our territory!"

"Not my problem. Where is the woman?"

"She's gone! She was gone days ago. You don't know what it's like in that hallway!"

"That is not my problem, either. I was promised an adult and I didn't receive one. You lied to me. Deceived us. That won't stand."

Acker looked over at a large, red-haired man in his group. The man grabbed Emily by the back of her head and walked her to the burning barrel in Denver's hallway. I moved to intervene, yet again, because this could only be brutal, could only end one way, but Dillon shot his arm out and shook his head. We had our own problems. We had been down to quarter rations for days. We were boiling clothing, eating leather. We needed to pick our battles, and we weren't even a part of this war.

The red-haired man shoved Emily at Acker, who caught her by her hair. Emily screamed as Acker pushed her head down toward the barrel.

"Stop! Just stop, we will get you what we promised, I swear it!" John Pollock yelled as a woman held him back and another KC-en took a shot at his ribs. "Please, don't hurt her, I swear, we give you twice what we promised for the books!"

"It's too late for that. Denver betrayed our arrangement and Emily Pollock speaks for Denver. Therefore Emily Pollock will take the punishment."

Acker shoved Emily's head deeper into the barrel and we heard the hiss of flame meeting skin and the smell of burning hair. Emily didn't scream, she moaned, the sort of moan a dying animal makes as it's being consumed but still lives to feel the viscera being ripped from its body.

"Please! Please stop!" John yelled again, tears running down his face. Dillon looked away but I had to watch. I spoke for Minneapolis. I had to watch. For them.

"Pity. You were really quite pretty. Can't imagine what you look like now. Should we finish it? Burn you in this barrel? Your group will be warm for days, wont they? A leader should sacrifice for her people."

Emily moaned again, but still she fought him with her legs, kicking and jabbing. Acker laughed, pulled her head out of the barrel, and threw her back against the wall. Her hair was burned away from the front half of her head. Her skin was melted, curled, and grotesque. But she lived.

"So," Acker started, and helped Natalie tie a long cord over the ceiling beam that ran above the desk. "Who speaks for Denver?"

The people in the hallways said nothing. John was docile, limp, as if all hope was lost, his daughter already dead. "Well, come on, tell me." Acker insisted, climbing on top of the desk and securing the cord while Natalie had somehow expertly tied into a noose. "Who speaks for you? Is it Emily Pollock? She'll be dead within days with those injuries and she knows it. So. Is it her?"

Silence. And then: *"Memmer ather."*

We all heard it, we all heard Emily try to speak as her bulging eyes watched Natalie twirl the noose. Acker jumped down from the desk and squatted in front of her, hands on his knees.

"Seems you're the only one willing to make a decision, cherry pie. So I'll ask you. Who speaks for Denver?"

"My...urer."

"Again, sweetheart, and speak up."

"Mer fauer."

"Are you saying your father?"

Emily nodded weakly. John lifted his head, the expression on his face one I can't even describe. Pain. Total devastation. His daughter was selling him out when she had no hope to live for herself.

"Disgusting," Mack whispered beside me.

Acker rose. "Do you agree?" He asked the rest of Denver, who still cowered against the wall in the hallway. "Is it John Pollock that speaks for you?"

At first no one moved. But then there were a few nods and weak agreements. Acker shrugged. "So be it." He nodded to the woman holding John and she dragged him toward the table. John didn't fight, didn't seem to want to escape his fate.

Natalie and the red-haired man hoisted John on top of the table and put the noose around his neck. Dillon was shaking next to me and I turned him away, pushed him toward Gracie, who caught him in her arms but she continued to watch the lynching.

Acker addressed the rest of the room. "Promises are very important in survival situations. They are often the difference between life and death. Denver betrayed us and John Pollock will die for that. This is a lesson to everyone still alive. Do not *fuck* with Kansas City." Acker leaned in close to John and told him something not meant for the entire room to hear. But I heard it. "Once you're dead, we're going to eat you. And then we're going to eat your daughter."

John remained stoic, unmoving and unspeaking as Acker hopped down from the desk. With no ceremony at all Natalie and the red-haired man pushed the desk out from under John.

The rope dropped half a foot and grew taut. John kicked and wheezed, and pulled at the noose around his neck. It lasted full minutes - several until he stopped moving. And I watched it all.

*

Emily died the next day. From what we heard she'd never spoken again, her last words the ones that ordered her own father's execution. In further penance for their crimes, Kansas City had taken all of Denver's books and wood and half of their remaining food which left them with one packs of nuts for 12 people. They began to die, one by one over the next three days. Most were sick already, like Salt Lake, and as they died the bodies were either tossed out into the snow or hauled away by Kansas City, depending on if they died of sickness or starvation.

"We're dying." Mack told me one night. "Some of us wont last to the end of tomorrow."

"I know," I said. "But I don't know what to do about it." I said and the scratch of Dillon's pencil stopped when the words left my mouth.

"Yes, you do." Dillon said.

"I'm open to suggestions. What do we do then?"

"Whatever we have to." Gracie told me, a surprisingly amount of fire in her words for as weak and broken as we all were. "I did not survive *everything* that happened in my life only to die in a fucking bus station."

216

"What do you guys want to do? Eat people? Is that it? You want to become cannibals like Kansas City?"

"It's not just Kansas City," Gracie said. "It's Salt Lake, too." She nodded toward the wall that had once supported over 20 people. But now there were only 13. I was starving, I was unfocused, I hadn't noticed. But it was true. I watched in horror as a man from Salt Lake carved strips of flesh out of a dead woman's leg and handed it over to another woman and what looked like her daughter They draped the pieces over a metal rod above the meager fire they could afford and watched them cook.

I rose and walked went to talk to the man with the pocket knife. "You're eating the dead." I accused him.

"Yeah." He said, without bothering to look up at me. "Amanda is allowing this?"

The man wiped his face on his sleeve. His eyes were runny. They were also blank of emotion. "Amanda's dead."

"When?" I asked quickly.

"This morning."

"But how could you.. Why would... She would never have wanted this." I insisted. "It goes against your *humanity*. It goes against-"

"She's the one who insisted upon it." He said and then gestured to the body he was carving. And it was her. There was a t-shirt draped over her face but I would have recognized her long, auburn hair, now dull and brittle, anywhere.

I stumbled back. "Christ."

Mack grabbed my arm and dragged me back to our camp. He shoved me into a chair. "Son. Listen to me. We can't *afford* humanity anymore. Those people want to survive. And so do ours."

"You're saying we should...we should just..."

"I'm saying that I'm dying here anyway, so I wont. But you should. *They* should," he said, gesturing back to our sick and dying group of bus mates.

"You're not gonna die here, Mack." I protested.

"Yes, I will. Maybe we all will. But you should at least try for it. You've got something to live for, don't you?"

I swallowed. My mouth was dry. My lips were cracked

"Who is it that you call everyday?"

"Mel." I answered. "Melody. My girlfriend. She- she's pregnant. With my kid."

"A family? That's enough. That's worth living for." He nodded sadly.

"What about you, Mack? Who's that letter for? What's in Post Falls?"

Mack leaned back in his seat and smiled, the first time in weeks. "My daughter."

"Yeah? You got grandkids, too?"

The smile fell a little. "I don't know. She wouldn't say." He was quiet for a moment. "I was a dumb kid. Knocked up a girl a knew. Nice girl. But I didn't want to be tied down. I left her some money and my car and I spilt. Never came back. Never saw her again. Thought about my kid a lot over the years. Finally did some digging about ten years ago, found out I had a little girl. Elaine. She's in her 40's now. Took me a decade to gather up the courage to reach out to her. She was mad." He laughed, a brittle sound. "She's still mad, not that I blame her. After a couple years of me bothering her every few days she agreed to meet me. In Post Falls. Just her. If she has kids, she don't want me around them, and I don't blame her for that either. I don't deserve to know my grandkids."

I was silent for a few minutes, thinking about Mack when I'd met him and how desperately he'd wanted to make his connections and get to Post Falls on time. "You're gonna meet her, Mack."

"What I'm gonna do is finish my letter before I die. And when I go you have permission to use my body to fuel yours."

"Fuck, Mack."

"I have faith in you, Romeo." He said, and patted me on the shoulder before laying down on the floor to sleep. Mack slept a lot these days.

*

"Denver is gone." "What?"

"Denver is gone." Gracie repeated. "The last four decided they'd rather die making a run for it than expire here against a wall and be eaten. I watched them all leave an hour ago."

I nodded my head. "That I can understand."

"Kris, we have decisions to make. When I was in the bathroom I heard Kansas City through the wall. I *heard* them say that the people dying of natural causes had no muscle and it wasn't enough to eat. They were arguing."

"Arguing about what?"

"About who in their group to sacrifice for food."

"In their own group?"

"Yes. Kris, things are really bad. They're cannibalizing themselves because they aren't getting enough meat off the dead."

"We've been starving for a month. Maybe more. I don't even know how long it's been."

"I know." She said. " But we're out of food. Completely. The peanut shells, the leather, everything is gone. We have to do what we have to do to survive."

"I know."

"Hey Stikes," Dillon interrupted. He sat down next to Gracie and gaze me a long look. "We, ah. We lost somebody last night."

"What? Who? Who did we lose?" I asked.

"Miles."

I ran my hands down my face. "Fuck."

"He wasn't eating all his rations back when we had food. He was trying to make sure there was enough for Dan and his mom."

"Aw, fuck, Miles."

"We need to...before he died Miles explained to me how to...prepare meat for consumption."

I heard him. I knew what he was saying. I looked around the 11 remaining members of my group. We wouldn't last much long. Miles was only the first. "Okay," I sighed. "Do it."

*

It happened at what I can only assume was night. The fire barrels were burning low. More people were asleep than awake. In fact, we had long given up the idea of sentries. No one could stay awake more than an hour anymore. Our bodies were shutting down.

I woke up to screams. Half-hearted, weak ones from my own group. It didn't take long to figure out what was wrong.

The entire Salt Lake City group had been slaughtered while everyone slept. Most of them had their throats cut, their necks draining blood onto the floor. Kansas City's door was wide open. I could see the bodies being harvested inside. I stumbled to my feet and crossed the long room to the door. I could sense Dillon and Gracie at my back. I saw Acker immediately. He was standing over a grill - an entire webber grill - flipping pieces of meat over with a fork. Everything smelled of dead flesh. Paper plates full of meat lined book shelves. The scene was absurd.

"You murdered them?" Was the only thing I managed to push through my teeth.

"Hey, Stikes. Yeah, we found this thing in the closet. A whole webber grill! Better than the garbage cans Salt Lake was cooking over, right?"

"You murdered them!" I launched myself at Acker, ready to tear him apart, but the red- haired guy caught me in the chin with a fist. I went down against the wall. Dillon helped me back up.

"Easy. Place nice." Acker handed the fork over to some-one else in his group and approached me casually, hands in his pockets. "It was mostly a waste, you know. A lot of those peo-ple were sick. And those that weren't barely have any meat on them. They weren't going to survive, Stikes. Most of them had only hours left. What we did was humane."

"None of this is humane! How many people have you murdered in this station by now?"

"We're surviving, man. Look around. Look at our group. We're alive, not at death's door. Nobody's running a marathon but we're more healthy than your people. And the other groups. We do what we do to survive. At the end of the day we're all animals. Would you blame an animal for killing to survive?"

"Animals aren't people."

"No. But people are animals. And you're starting to figure that out. We saw. Last night we saw you. Your people were cutting up that kid in the jets jacket. You're gonna eat him. It was always gonna come to that. You should have done it sooner. Now it's too late, just like Salt Lake."

"Is that a threat?"

"Maybe it would have been. But judging by what we're getting off of these fucking people it wouldn't be worth it."

"Let me ask you something, Acker, what's the point of surviving if you lose your humanity?"

He leaned into me and I could smell the stench of the people on his breath. "That's easy. Surviving."

I stared at him as he reached back and pulled a strip of meat from a paper plate and held it out to me. I tightened my jaw and he smiled, shoving it into his mouth and chewing, never breaking eye contact with me.

"Come on, Kris, let's go." Gracie whispered.

*

The smell of cooking meat was strong. It permeated the entire building by now. As much as I hated it, my mouth watered and my mind could think of little else. Miles had been stripped and prepared. The meat was cooking nearby. Dan watched it excitedly as did other members of my group. My only request had been that Dillon and the others harvest the body away from the site of our little camp. But Dan was a smart kid and he probably knew. But he was beyond caring. Most of us were.

The meat was passed around, but I declined. I'd known Miles. Talked to him. Strategized with him. I knew he'd been on the way home from college for Thanksgiving break. He was excited about seeing his mom and his twin brother. So when the makeshift scrap of metal serving as a plate got to me, I passed it on. Yes, I was starving. But this was a person. And me? I couldn't eat a person. Especially not someone I knew.

Kansas City kept their door cracked most of the time to allow the smoke from the webber to escape. Sometimes we would hear arguments, sometimes out and out brawling before things would go quiet again.

Mack didn't work on his letter much anymore. He spent a lot of time listening to Dillon talk about Sarah. Mack had a fondness for young love, I think. Gracie hung out with Dan a lot as his mother was getting weaker and sicker by the day. She had also passed on the meat, though she encouraged Dan to eat his fill and forbid anyone from admitting what it actually was. Or who. Dan had liked Miles.

For my part, I still called Melody everyday and told her I was always right here. I also told her I was sorry that I was never going home, that I'd never see her again, know our child, get to watch how great of a mother she would become.

Time was strange. It drifted by in unfamiliar increments. Hunger was constant. The cold relentless. Even the fires seemed to lose much of their heat as the hours passed.

We were out of meat from Miles's body on the first day. Then an older man, Harry, died in his sleep. His wife told us it was his wish to contribute. So we cooked him and ate him, too. Except for me. I couldn't bring myself to eat a man in front of his wife.

And then came the last day. The very last day we spent at Whitefall. Who knew what day that was.

It started with a lot of yelling. It was Acker, of course, and some of his people. A kid who couldn't have been more than 18 ran out of the employee breakroom. He seemed to be going for the front door, but Acker caught him, and threw him on the floor.

"You know the rules, Clarkson, you've been enjoying them long enough." He turned to Natalie. "Get the hammer."

I rose to my feet, shaky and weak. I hadn't eaten anything but leather in days. But whatever was about to happen would be bad. If I was going to die anyway, maybe I could stop it. Stop this one bad thing from happening.

"What are you doing?" I asked as I reached them. Acker did a table take and then started laughing.

"Holy shit, Stikes, is that you? You look fucking horrible!" Acker chuckled as I pushed my way into the middle of the melee.

"What is all this? What are you doing to this kid?"

Acker shrugged. "Nothing to do with you."

"I want to know anyway."

"Sure you wouldn't rather just tottle along? Go finish dying in the corner?"

"What are you going to do to him?"

"Well, see, in the Kansas City group we have a rule about the greater good. And whatever the greatest good is that you can offer the group, well, that's what you're gonna do."

"And what is his *greatest good*?" I spat.

Acker took the hammer from Natalie and pointed it at the kid. "His meat. That's all he's got left to offer at this point."

Gracie's voice rang out from behind me. "You're going to kill a perfectly healthy person for their *meat*?"

Natalie laughed. "Oh honey, it wouldn't be the first time."

"You've been cannibalizing your own group?" I asked Acker.

"We're surviving, aren't we?"

"You've fucking snapped, Acker. That kid can't be more than 19!" I yelled. "Pick an older person!"

"Our older people have other skills we can use. He doesn't. Anyway, this isn't a debate, Stikes, I've satisfied your curiosity, now fuck off. Boomer, hold him down."

The large, red-haired man flipped the kid over and sat on his back, holding his head between his meaty hands. The kid screamed bloody, terrified murder. I don't think I've ever heard more fear in a voice before or since. It was all too much for me.

As Acker turned toward the kid I rushed him from behind and sucker punched him in the back of the head. He went down, and the hammer skittered across the floor. They were on me in an instant. Kicking, punching, fuck, even biting. And I couldn't fight back. I was big guy, but I was thin now, drained of energy. I didn't have the strength. I heard Mack there, fighting, trying to pull them off of me. Mack wasn't a great fighter in the best of times but now, days from his death...

I heard them beat him, I felt them beat me. At one point I was lying on the floor looking across it, getting kicked from behind. Mack was in the fetal position, covering his head. Gracie was trying to get to him, throwing punches of her own. She really was a little scrapper, but the hits seemed louder when they made contact with her body. I tried to call them off, call them *all* off. But no sounds came out of me. That's where my memories end.

*

I woke up to someone dumping water down my throat. It was Dillon. I was on my back on the floor in our camp. I would recognize those ceiling tiles anywhere. I'd been staring at them for what felt like years.

"Take it easy. You got it pretty bad." Dillon said. I sat up anyway with great effort. My vision was blurred and my mind was slow. Everything fucking hurt.

"Gracie." I croaked.

"She's okay. A little banged up but she's tough."

I nodded. That sounded like her. He handed the bottle to me and I took another sip of water. "And Mack?"

Dillon didn't respond. I looked over at him but he was looking out the window, at the pane of black snow. "And Mack?" I asked, louder this time.

"Mack...Mack was hours away from dying, anyway,

Kris." "And...did he?"

Dillon nodded. "The fight was too much for him."

"Fuck. No, Mack. Not you." I moaned.

"He said to tell you that he finished his letter."

I pushed my palms into my eyes. "Where is it?"

"I put it in your backpack. Seemed like you would know what to do with it."

"Right. And everyone else?"

"They're scared. But... they seem a little stronger. They're eating…"

"Who?"

Dillon said nothing.

"Harry?"

Dillon took a deep breath. "Speaking of... you need to eat, Kris."

"What about the kid. From Kansas City. Did he…"

Dillon shook his head. "They were never going to let him leave. You know that."

"So he died anyway. After all that."

"Yeah."

"And I got Mack killed, too."

"Mack was done for anyway. You know that."

I said nothing and drank more water. Gracie was nearby, I could hear her singing to Dan. At least I hadn't gotten her killed. Only by the grace of God, though, I was fairly sure God had long ago abandoned Whitefall.

"Kris, you need to eat. You're weak. You body needs to repair itself."

I looked down at the plate in Dillon's lap. It was filled with chunks of gray meat that smelled like rot and death. But also made me salivate with need. "I can't." I said.

"I heard what you said to Mack. About your girl and your baby. Have you ever told Melody that you would do anything for her?"

My eyes snapped to his face. "Fuck you."

"Would you do anything for your kid? He or she is going to need you. Melody is going to need you."

"Is that why you do it?" I asked him."For Sarah?"

Dillon was quiet for a minute. "No, not for Sarah. There is no Sarah. There never was. I do it for Sam."

"There is no Sarah." I repeated.

"Everything I told you was true. But, about Sam, not Sarah." He took a breath. "I love him."

I looked down at the meat he was holding. He really must. To do this. To go against nature. Everything that made him human. He did it for Sam.

I lifted my eyes to his face. "Sam who loves mountains."

Dillon nodded and his eyes fell back to the meat.

"He sounds great, man."

Dillon smiled a little at that and offered the plate to me again. "Do it for her. Do it for them."

I let out a long, slow breath.

"You know Mack would smack you upside the head if you didn't."

I wanted to laugh but it wasn't in me. Mack had never eaten someone he'd known. He'd died before having to suffer that indignity. I knew what I was eating. I had a good idea of *who* I was eating. And I couldn't do it.

But...it didn't matter if I couldn't. Because I had to. I was starving. I was *dying*. Mack died for me. Mel needed me.

Our baby needed me. So, I reached over and picked up a chuck of silvery meat. It was well-done and looked like it was cut for a stew. The smell was sickening, but saliva filled my mouth just the same. I set the cube inside and began to chew. It was tough, and tasteless but I still swallowed it practically whole. I took another piece and ate that. Then another and another. Then I was rabid, feral. Fucking *starving*.

I saw him, as I consumed more and more of the meat. Acker. Standing in the doorway of his room. Watching me. A smug smile on his face. But I didn't care. I ate until only one piece of meat remained. And as I reached down to take it, the cackle of the PA popped overhead. Some of us screamed in shock, others gasped. Then we all fell silent.

"Good evening, folks. I've got good news! The storm has let up and the snow has been dug away from the bay doors. We're gonna get you on out of here within the next 30 minutes so please check the overhead board in the terminal and line up at the corresponding doorway to your bus. I know many of you are making bus changes in Whitefall so please be sure to double-check your ticket before lining up. Our drivers have the busses warming up for you as we speak and we will all be on our way in a few minutes. We'd like to thank you for your patience during this delay."

It was over. It was over and we were leaving.

The power in the station suddenly clicked back on and we were washed in bright, white light. And in it, we could see our crimes more fully. The half-eaten bodies. The pools of blood. The glass. The broken things. Our sunken cheeks and the ribs in our chest. The gray piece of meat in front of me, once my friend. I could see the sinewy strings of muscle. And I ate that last piece right then. Because we were leaving, but I was still hungry.

We all rose, picked up what was left of our bags, and checked the board in a trance. I was at door 4. Dillon was at 2. Gracie, 1. We stood next to each other as we read the board. And we stared at each other as we got in our respective lines. But no one spoke. There was nothing to say. Not even good-bye.

All I had left in my bag was Mack's letter, some scraps of clothing, and $6 in cash. In a daze, I watched the bay door open and dug in my pocket for my ticket, which was still there, after all these weeks, now bloody and torn.

Richard, our bus driver from before, took my ticket and punched it without a word. I boarded the bus and took a window seat facing the station. There were only a handful of people on the bus. Everyone else was dead or lost. We were all in shock, not quite believing it was real, that we were escaping, that we weren't going to die in Whitefall.

As we pulled away from the terminal I noticed that the blizzard was over and I could see for miles. There was no town beyond the bus station. There never had been. Those that had ventured out had never returned. They were lost in the white nothingness.

I felt a body fall into the seat next to me and my eyes snapped over to find Acker shoving his ticket back into his backpack. "Hey, Stikes, didn't think you'd be on my bus. You headed to Seattle, too?"

I stared at him. "Spokane."

"Nice. I've going to see my girlfriend. My family lives there, too, but Thanksgivings at my dad's are always un-fuckin-pleasant because of his wife. I didn't even tell them I was coming. Just gonna hide out at my girl's house."

I didn't respond.

"You going to see your girl?"

"My family." I answered, my words slow.

"Ah, sucks to be you, then." He unzipped the top of his bag and dug around a bit and then pulled out a king size Milky Way. "Want one? I have a couple."

I stared at the candy bar. "You had fucking candy?"

Acker shrugged. "I was saving it. It's my favorite." I tore it out of his hands and stood, then pushed against his legs to get out. "Name's Luke, by the way." He said.

I didn't answer, just moved to the back of the bus and sat in an empty row. I tore into the candy bar and it was gone in under a minute.

The first stop we made with a fast food restaurant, I got off   and bought the 3 biggest things on the dollar menu and then filled my water bottle for free. I couldn't think bout the events at whitefall. My body told me to eat, rest, eat, Mel. Whitefall would get it's time later.

The first thing thing I did when I got the receipt was glance at the date. It was Tuesday the 20th. Two days before Thanksgiving. That would mean we were only at Whitefall for one night. One. Night. It was impossible.

I ran straight to the payphone on the outside of the building, inserted the quarters I had made sure to get as change, and dialed Mandy's number.

"Hello?"

"Mel?"

"Hey, baby. Where are you?"

"Mel, when was the last time you talked to me?"

"What?" She asked, confusion in her voice.

"When was the last time I called?"

"Um, yesterday? The connection was bad, I was trying to tell you about my doctor's appointment. Did you hear me? The line was really crap."

I tried to breathe deeply. "Yeah, baby, I heard you."

"Good. How's the trip?"

"Mel, did you hear what I said? Yesterday?"

"Yes. You told me you loved me and that you were always there."

"Yeah. And I am, Mel."

"I know."

"I would do anything for you. For you and our daughter."

"Oh, it's a girl now?" She laughed.

"Yeah. I really think it is."

I heard the driver whistle then and told Mel I loved her again and that I would call her from Billings.

I tried to stagger the burgers so that I wouldn't make myself sick. I was still starving and weak. The first burger almost made me throw up. I ate half a burger every few hours after that.

I was nervous about Post Falls. We arrived in the evening, close to 9. It was cold, but not as cold as the terminal at Whitefall had been. I clutched Mack's letter in my hand as I exited the bus. I saw her immediately. She had dark hair, and was short like Mack. But the thing that stopped me dead were the kids in her arms. A toddler on her hip and a little boy holding her hand. And he looked a whole lot like his grandfather. I took a deep breath.

The woman looked nervous but excited. She rocked from foot to foot and a man behind her rubbed her shoulder and whispered into her ear. I was glad he was there. She would need the support after I gave her the letter.

I walked over to Mack's daughter and waited for her to notice me. But she didn't even see me, so intent was she on watching the stairs of the bus. "Elaine?"

She started and her eyes shot to mine. Her eyebrows pinched in confusion. "Yes?" I held the letter out to her. "This is from your father."

She took it slowly, and then glanced back at the bus. "Where is he?"

"He, ah... He really wanted to come."

It was all I could say, I could only hope that Mack had told her the rest.

"He's not coming?" Tears filled her eyes.

"No. But he really, really wanted to, Elaine. More than he wanted anything else."

"I..I don't understand."

I nodded at the paper in her hands. "Read the letter." I turned and headed toward the payphones.

"Wait!" She called. I turned back to her. "Do you know my father?"

"I'd like to think so" I shrugged. "Maybe. He never told me his real name."

She was quiet a moment. "Arthur Warren MacKenzie."

I nodded.

"Thank you for the letter." She said, and then turn back to her husband. I walked toward the phone bank, ready to call my girl. "You were wrong, Mack. Your whole family was here waiting for you."

*

When I got off the bus in Spokane, I didn't turn around. Acker was still on it, though he spent most of his time listening to his headphones and playing pocket poker. My walkman was long gone, fed to the fire weeks ago.

But then, I changed my mind. I climbed back onto the bus, walked right to his seat, didn't wait for him to see me and punched him in the face240, then kneed him in the nuts. I used his hair to jerk his face upright. His nose was already bleeding.

"How's that for playing nice, Acker?"

I threw him onto the floor while Richard the bus driver yelled at me to get off, promising I'd never ride a Greyloor bus again.

My family was there to meet me at the Spokane terminal. They took me home. I ate, rested, and eventually got my strength back. My uncles gave me a job, I worked it three weeks and then used the money to buy a ticket for my girl. A *plane* ticket.

Mel gave birth to our daughter in May. We named her Amanda Gracie Stikes.

The bus company thought I was crazy when I called when I called to "complain". They told me there was no station in Whitefall. In fact, there are *no* stops between Fargo and Great Falls, Montana. Furthermore, they said, there was no city called Whitefall anywhere in the continental US.

Since my ticket was long gone, there was no way to prove it had been real. Other than the deaths. And I often wondered about those missing persons investigations, and where it had led the detectives. If there was no Whitefall, there was nowhere to look. They must have decided all those people had simply vanished into thin air. And maybe they had.

I try not to think about Whitefall, anymore, thirty years later, but it's there at night. In my dreams, the ones that turn to nightmares. I never really escaped. Because I aways go back. And in my dreams, I always will.

The End?

Of course not.